D1527764

Egyptian and Sudanese
Folk-tales

Egyptian and Sudanese Folk-tales

Retold by
HELEN MITCHNIK

Illustrated by
ERIC FRASER

1478
1978

OXFORD UNIVERSITY PRESS
OXFORD NEW YORK TORONTO

Oxford University Press, Walton Street, Oxford OX2 6DP

OXFORD LONDON GLASGOW
NEW YORK TORONTO MELBOURNE WELLINGTON
IBADAN NAIROBI DAR ES SALAAM CAPE TOWN
KUALA LUMPUR SINGAPORE JAKARTA HONG KONG TOKYO
DELHI BOMBAY CALCUTTA MADRAS KARACHI

British Library Cataloguing in Publication Data

Mitchnik, Helen
Egyptian and Sudanese folk-tales.
1. Tales, Sudanese   2. Tales, Egyptian
I. Title   II. Fraser, Eric
398.2'1'09624   GR355.8   78-40202

ISBN 0-19-274122-5

*Printed in Great Britain by
Lowe & Brydone Printers Limited,
Thetford, Norfolk*

Contents

Introduction *vii*

Destiny *1*

The sultan and the cobbler *14*

Different times have different 'adans' *21*

'O luck of the ugly . . .' *22*

The man who did not believe in luck *28*

The poor man's bowl *31*

A discerning old 'faki' *37*

The old crone who was more wily
than Iblees *39*

Wise sayings for a thousand dinars each *46*

The rashness of the young and the
wisdom of the old *54*

The farmer who found his match in his
daughter-in-law *62*

The eye will see what it is destined to see . . . *71*

The fisherman and the prince *79*

The ten white doves *85*

Hassan the physician *93*

Hassan the brave *100*

Karakosh and Goha *109*

To my nephews and nieces —
both eastern and western

Introduction

The collection of folk-tales in this book has been drawn from my childhood memories of the Sudan and my travels, in later years, throughout Upper and Lower Egypt.

At that time the Sudan was just emerging from the rigidity of the Mahdi's rule, during the fourteen years of which, every sort of festivity and amusement was strictly taboo. Indeed, even throughout the whole of my adolescent years in the Sudan, present-day diversions in the way of theatres, cinemas, recreation-centres and the like, were non-existent.

Therefore, when the day's chores were over, and daylight turned to dusk, people would resort for relaxation and entertainment to the age-old custom of story-telling, or *huja*, as it is called in the Sudan.

Story-telling was quite an art in my time. It was practised with true craftsmanship, and prevailed amongst all shades of the Arabic speaking community: from the rich in their gilded salons, to the poor in their humble *tukuls* (mud-huts); and from the tradespeople in bazaars and market-places, to the nomad in the desert, and the beggar who came to the door.

All of these stories are oral traditions of the past, inherited by children and grandchildren from successive generations of forbears, and crystallized by constant repetition into the form in which we know them today.

Not all of them are purely for entertainment. Many are an example of constructive thinking, and many are a lesson in social morality, ranking high in which, is respect for parents and elders; honesty and integrity in person-to-person dealings; non-betrayal of trust; concern for the stranger in our midst; and last, though in no way least, the triumph of good over evil.

Introduction

As a child, folk-tales were the bedtime stories on which I was put to sleep; and though most of them fairly bristled with exploits of *jinn* and *ghoul*, and *ifreet* (demon), my peaceful slumber was thereby in no way disturbed. For *jinn* and *ghoul* and *ifreet* hold no terror for the Sudanese. They are merely 'characters' on the familiar stage of day-to-day life, and reference to them is made openly, freely, and without fuss or fear.

Yet no man in his right senses would ever dare venture alone, after dark, past a graveyard or a derelict house or forsaken well, for these are considered to be the favourite haunt of evil spirits who fill the atmosphere around us. And invisible though they are, they could appear whenever they chose. A *jinn* could then 'ride' a man and rob him of his mental and physical faculties, or indeed, destroy him altogether. *Jinn yirkabak* (may a *jinn* 'ride' you), is an expletive which springs all too readily to the lips of a Sudanese.

One other deeply rooted tradition in the Sudan and Egypt, is the absolute belief in destiny, or *al-maktoob*, as it is currently known. Thus, from the cradle to the grave, every move we make on the chessboard of life, is subject to the irrefutable laws of *al-maktoob*. No one can alter it. No one can evade it. 'You are led, you are not given to choose, O son of Adam'; or, 'What is written on the forehead, the eye is bound to see', are two uncontested truths throughout the entire Arabic speaking world.

Hand in hand with the belief in *al-maktoob*, goes the belief in the element of luck. For, without it, notwithstanding any resourcefulness or cleverness you may possess, you could still fail to succeed. Whereas, given luck, irrespective of whether or not you are resourceful or clever, were you to play with sand, it could turn to gold in your hands. Hence, the all too popular saying: Give me an ounce of luck, rather than a *feddan* of cleverness.

Introduction

In like manner, given the choice, a lady of unprepossessing appearance would sooner be lucky than rich. For, if luck 'stood' for her, she would shine forth like the moon in its fourteenth night in the eyes of a male suitor.

Conversely, luck 'stands' for an ugly suitor too. Wealth on its own may not always further his advances. In this connection there is a spicy little Arabic proverb: 'Do not take the monkey for his wealth, the wealth will go and the monkey will remain himself.'

There are, of course, many more traditional and superstitious beliefs in the Sudan and Egypt, such as the all too popular belief in the Evil Eye, and the power of magic. But these are too diversified and complicated topics to be included in this introduction.

I will, therefore, by-pass them and tell you of the mystical figure seven which, for some unknown reason, has a magic of its own in the Arabic speaking countries.

You will note that seven recurs in a repetitive pattern throughout the stories in this book: a *jinn* has seven heads, another has seven lives, the lives are contained in seven little green birds, a brave man wields seven swords, and festivities are held during seven days and seven nights.

Festivities are still held for seven days and seven nights in our present-day Arab world; a much travelled man is said to have crossed the seven seas; a transport of joy sends us to the seventh heaven of happiness; and our *Suboo* (the seventh day of our birth or death), is of significant importance in our life. It is celebrated in style, with the rejoicings due to one, and the solemnity due to the other.

Apart from all this, the Sudanese and Egyptians are, on the whole, an easy-going fun-loving people. The pace of their life is unhurried and leisurely, and their hospitality is proverbial. A man would 'pawn his wife', so to speak, rather than forgo the code of hospitality to a guest for lack of ready funds.

They also have a subtle sense of humour, immortalized in characters like 'Goha' and 'Abu Nawas', anecdotes of which could fill volumes.

In conclusion, I would like to introduce you to the most current word in the Arabic language: the word *inshallah,* (God willing).

You can sow and reap, you can buy and sell, you can build and plan, you can come and go; but it has all to be subject to *inshallah.*

However if, like Goha, you decide to do away with *inshallah,* then, like Goha, you must suffer the consequence:

'Where are you off to, Goha?' said a friend to him one morning.

'I am off to market to buy me a cow,' said Goha.

'Gul "inshallah",' (say 'inshallah') said the friend.

'Why *should* I say "inshallah",' said Goha. 'The money is in my pocket, the cow is in the market. What's to prevent me from buying it?'

On that the two men parted. Later in the day they met again.

'Well, Goha,' said the friend, 'where's the cow?'

Said Goha, 'inshallah, I lost the money.'

And so, on this nostalgic note of happy memories, I leave you to read, and, inshallah, enjoy these stories.

H.M.

Destiny

In a little village bordering a vast land over which a Sultan reigned and ruled, there once lived a venerable old man and his name was Sheikh Ramadan.

He feared God and shunned all evil. And he had a large family of sons and daughters for whom he was the sole provider. But due to his declining years, and the fact that he could no longer find a ready market for the charms and amulets he made, and on which he solely depended for his livelihood, it was becoming harder and harder for him to feed so many hungry mouths all on his own.

His wife didn't spare him either. She lashed at him with her tongue, reviling and denigrating him for his impotence to provide for his family, and threatening time and again to return to her own people where, she declared, she would at least be certain of going to bed with a full warm belly.

The Sheikh took it all very patiently at first, but when the situation became intolerable, he decided that the best way out of his dilemma would be for him to get lost in the wilderness where some wild beast of prey, or the spirit of some roving *jinn* would be sure to destroy him. And much though this was against his religious principles, he would at least thereby ensure that when he was gone his children would be well looked after. For his wife would not leave them behind; she would take them along with her to her people, where they too would go to bed with a full warm belly.

As for him, he was already an old man. And the end could therefore not be too far. So what matter if he died a little sooner than was *maktoob*? In any case his death would be short and swift, for the Red Jinn who inhabited the Haunted Well in the wilderness brooked no trespassers. And no sooner would he smell him out, than he would extinguish his life's light.

Having thus taken this drastic decision, Sheikh Ramadan recited his customary prayers one evening, and when the moans and groans of his hungry children had subsided into the torpors of heavy sleep, he picked up his rosary and his staff, and stepped resolutely out into the night.

It was a dark wild night and a heavy storm was imminent. But Sheikh Ramadan's courage never wavered. He was intent on reaching the wilderness before break of dawn. So on he walked, for hour after hour, steadily thumbing his rosary.

Soon the sleepy little village lay far behind as he could tell by the dead stillness that wrapped itself around him. Presently the eerie laugh of a hyena sent cold shivers down his spine, and he began to feel oppressed as the silence around him seemed all at once to be alive with strange noises. In an agony of apprehension he paused to wipe his brow.

Suddenly he perceived a faint white glimmer in the distance detach itself from the thick blackness of night and move stealthily towards him. His knees shook, and his heart stood still. The Haunted Well! That faint white glimmer must be the spirit of the Jinn which constantly hovered around it. . . .

In a grip of deadly fear he turned to flee, for life is good, but a great crash of thunder sent him reeling to the ground.

'No!' he screamed, as he fell in a heap. 'I do not want to die. . . . I want to live. . . . Save me Almighty Allah. . . . I want to live. . . .'

And as if in answer to his anguished prayer, a voice from the dark came to him: 'Thou shalt live. Thou shalt live and prosper.'

Fearfully Sheikh Ramadan turned his head in the direction of the voice. Impenetrable darkness still hemmed him in, but a great glimmering ball of white cloud now stood close before him.

'Sheikh Ramadan,' continued the voice peremptorily, 'collect thyself and listen to me.'

Trembling in every limb the Sheikh struggled to his knees and asked feebly: 'Who art thou that speakest from the dark?'

'I am Destiny,' replied the voice, and thereat the great glimmering ball of white cloud fell apart revealing a woman – radiant and resplendent in all the glory of eternal youth and beauty. She was completely robed in shimmering white, and in her hand she held the golden sceptre which she wielded over the fate of all men.

'It is decreed that thou livest,' she proceeded to say, 'thou art not to die. Prosperity and fame and riches are to be thy lot; thou art to mingle with royalty, and thousands shall flock to thee and listen to thy words of wisdom, and marvel at thy foresight and thy prophecy. It is *maktoob*.'

Sheikh Ramadan stared at her in speechless wonder. He was still too stunned to grasp the full meaning of what she was saying, but the magic words, 'prosperity and fame and riches', kept ringing in his ears, and finally registered in his whirling brain.

Slowly life surged back in his veins. And with it, cold reason reasserted itself. 'Take heed!' it cautioned. 'Destiny has come to you today bringing the world to your feet. But for how long? For was she not known to be as callous and treacherous as she was kind and bountiful?'

Aloud he said: 'I bid thee a thousand welcomes. But hast thou come to me to stay?'

'Only for as long as it is *maktoob*.'

'And for how long is it *maktoob*?'

'That is not for mortal man to know, O son of Adam.'

'Then thou wilt leave me one day? Thou wilt plunge

me back into the sordid poverty and unending misery which have driven me to barter my life for my children's daily bread? If that is what for me is *maktoob*, then I refuse to accept it.'

'It is not for thee to accept or reject the *maktoob*,' was the stern rejoinder. 'Kind or cruel, bounteous or niggardly, what is *maktoob* must be fulfilled. Such is the destiny of all men. No one can escape it.'

'But how long will my prosperity last?' persisted the Sheikh desperately. 'And after it, what is to become of me?'

'*Maktoob*, O son of Adam,' was the implacable reply. 'It is all *maktoob,* and nothing I can say, and nothing thou canst do, would either modify or alter it in any way. Now get thee back to thy village, to thy home and thy children, and there await the fulfilment of what for thee is *maktoob*.'

Obediently Sheikh Ramadan rose to his feet. 'So be it,' he said. 'But thou canst at least promise me one thing: that before thou leavest me, thou wilt give me fair warning.'

'I promise thee,' said Destiny, and thereat the great glimmering ball of white cloud closed over her and swiftly receded into the blackness of night.

The sun was high up in the heavens when Sheikh Ramadan reached his native village, and hurried to his home, torn by a million doubts: Would Destiny really keep faith with him? Would he and his children never go hungry again? Would he really be prosperous and rich and famous?

With a trembling hand he pushed open the rickety wooden gate of his dusty small *hosh* (courtyard), and great was his joy when he saw that some of his prosperous neighbours had suddenly thought of calling on his wife, bringing with them generous gifts of flour and butter and milk and honey. The appetising aroma of freshly baked bread intoxicated him, and the sight of a

4

large gourd of creamy frothy milk from which his children drew long avid draughts brought a lump to his throat and tears of gratitude to his eyes. Allah be praised! Destiny was indeed keeping faith with him.

And so, the years of hunger and misery were slowly obliterated in a smooth serene stream of affluent days which succeeded each other.

Shortly after this, a gang of robbers broke into the Royal Palace and carried off the Sultan's safe with all his gold and silver.

The Sultan offered a reward of one thousand rials to anyone who could bring back the safe or lead to the discovery of the robbers. But though the pick of his Royal Guards was designated to search every house and draw out every well in the town and neighbouring villages, it was all of no avail. The earth seemed to have opened up and to have swallowed both robbers and safe.

In the meantime, the Sultan's wrath waxed higher and higher. Then, one day, in a last desperate attempt to recover his riches, he ordered his Vizier to round up all the sorcerers and seers in the land, and consult them about the robbery.

They came in their numbers. And any one of them who failed to throw some light on the whereabouts of the robbers or the safe, was promptly beheaded and his head hung on the Palace walls.

Soon ninety-nine heads were swinging, and the Sultan threatened that unless his safe were soon retrieved, his own Vizier's head would go to complete the hundred.

The Vizier panicked. His head was at stake. And he knew his liege well enough to be in no doubt that he would carry out his threat. He therefore doubled and redoubled his efforts in his search for the safe, and gave the soldiers of the Palace no peace over it. He moreover sent out town-criers to proclaim the 1000 rials reward to anyone who could lead to the recovery of the safe or the discovery of the robbers, threatening at the same time to reek the most horrible vengeance on all and sundry for failing to do so.

As the search grew hotter and hotter, the robbers became alarmed. The noose was now steadily tightening round their neck, and they therefore felt that it would be safer for them to move out of their present hide-out with their booty and bury it far out in the wilderness where even the Sultan's soldiers wouldn't dare venture.

There were forty of them. And so as to avoid detection, their leader ordered them to steal out of their hide-out one by one at dead of night and at regular intervals of a minute or so, between one and the other.

Now the way to the wilderness lay past Sheikh Ramadan's *hosh* wall. It was just before break of dawn and the night was at its darkest. But the Sheikh was already squatting on his prayer mat, and had just finished reciting the first of his forty rosaries when the first robber slunk past his *hosh* wall.

'Adi wahid!' (There goes one!), called out the Sheikh who kept count of the rosaries he recited by aiming a pebble at his *hosh* wall out of a little mound of forty pebbles he kept by him.

The robber, thinking he had been detected, froze in his tracks. After what seemed an interminable time he heard the faint echo of the second robber's footsteps stealthily approaching, and breathed a sigh of relief: all was well. The old man must have been dreaming.

But no sooner did the second robber come up to the *hosh* wall than Sheikh Ramadan called out: 'Adi itnein!' (Here goes two!), aiming at the same time a second pebble at his *hosh* wall.

The robber instantly hugged the wall for shelter, and

stood alongside his mate, shivering with the terror of detection.

Presently the third robber was heard stealthily approaching. And here again, no sooner did he reach the *hosh* wall than Sheikh Ramadan called out: 'Adi talata!' (Here goes three!), aiming his third pebble at the *hosh* wall.

And so it went on. Every time one of the robbers came up to the *hosh* wall, he would hear himself being loudly counted by the Sheikh, and his presence behind the wall clearly emphasized by the pebble which struck it.

So that when the fortieth robber – who was also the leader of the gang, arrived just as Sheikh Ramadan called out conclusively: 'Wi adi arba'een!' (And here goes forty!), he didn't have to be told that the game was up. But rather than be beheaded or impaled on the Palace gates, he decided to give himself and his gang up, and plead with the Sheikh for mercy.

So, one by one the robbers jumped over the *hosh* wall, hauling the heavy safe between them, and prostrated themselves on the ground before the praying Sheikh. They kissed his hands and embraced his knees, and after begging him not to denounce them to the Sultan, they melted swiftly away in the dark.

Soon the pearly light of dawn began to illumine the night sky. Sheikh Ramadan, still greatly bewildered by what had happened, peered closer at the object at his feet. And great was his stupefaction when he realized that it was the Sultan's safe – the safe for which all the Sultan's soldiers and seers had searched in vain. It was here, at his very feet. Now indeed he will be a rich man. Now indeed the 1000 rials reward will be his; and he will be able to buy that much coveted ass and ride him in comfort to all the neighbouring villages. Now, too, he will be able to buy a cow, and his children will never again go hungry. For milk and butter and cheese will be overflowing in his home. Again, all praise to Almighty Allah! Destiny was continuing to keep faith with him.

And so, Sheikh Ramadan went leisurely through his morning ablutions, and when the sun had risen clear above the thatched roofs of the village mud huts, he donned his white turban and clean caftan and took himself to the Sultan's Palace.

The Sultan listened in awe to the tale Sheikh Ramadan recounted to him, as to how the King of the Jinns – whom he had not ceased to invoke for the recovery of the Sultan's safe, had finally appeared to him in the night and revealed to him the hiding place of the safe.

He, however, warned the Sultan not to insist on knowing where that hiding place was, nor who the robbers were, for that was the secret of the King of the Jinns and he had no authority to divulge it.

The Sultan nodded his head in acquiescence. 'The wish of the King of the Jinns will be respected, my friend; and thou art not only to receive the 1000 rials reward for the recovery of the safe, but it is our royal wish that thou becomest our own personal seer and adviser, and that thou takest up quarters in our royal palace from this moment on.'

So saying, the Sultan struck his hands together, and to the army of slaves who sprang up like so many mushrooms around him, he consigned the bewildered Sheikh.

Immediately the Palace barber and tailor and cobbler were summoned, and they set to work on their man, shaving his head, trimming his beard, and fitting him out in the finest silks and linen, and the softest footwear. When they had finished, the transformation was so complete, that Sheikh Ramadan's own mother would not have recognized him.

The Sultan treated him with every consideration, and showered gifts and favours upon him. He also consulted him on all important matters of state, and Sheikh

Ramadan spoke as one inspired. Soon his fame spread far and wide, and people from all parts of the land came to seek his advice, and listen to his prophecy and his words of wisdom.

In the Palace his word was law, and he was held in equal awe and respect as the Sultan himself.

Thus he lived for many a long year, drinking his fill of the cup of happiness. His children were now grown up and happily married, and his wife was well looked after and secure. He hadn't a care in the world.

Then came the day when Iblees whispered in his ear that he still didn't know what was to befall him after his years of prosperity. Destiny had simply said: '*Maktoob*, O son of Adam. It is all *maktoob*, and nothing I can say, and nothing thou canst do, would either modify or alter it in any way.'

What was this part of the *maktoob* that he was not to know? Why had Destiny witheld it from him so stubbornly? A million doubts rose to assail him.

Destiny had also said: 'I will abide with thee only for as long as it is *maktoob*.' What if the *maktoob* were to terminate tomorrow? What would become of him then? He would lose his inspiration and would be proclaimed a fraud. He would be mercilessly stripped and chased out of the Palace, perhaps even thrown into a dungeon to rot away the rest of his life, or he might be beheaded and his head hung out on the Palace walls, meat for the crows.

He shuddered. No! None of this must happen to him. He would see to it. He would forestall Destiny and run away from the *maktoob* before it overtook him. But how? How could he run away from this hateful Palace which all of a sudden now seemed like a close prison to him? Where could he hide from the Sultan? Everybody knew him, and wherever he went they would find him and bring him back.

In a state of anguish he paced his rooms. Suddenly an

idea occurred to him: he would feign madness! Nobody would want him then, not even the Sultan. And he would be allowed to go his way, free and unmolested, for people, on the whole, were always kind to a madman.

It was then mid-morning. And the Sultan, immersed in a tubful of water, was having his morning bath surrounded by the usual retinue of slaves, some soaping him, some massaging him, some pouring scented water over his head, when suddenly the bathroom door flew open and an apparition burst in: half naked, hair dishevelled, eyes wild, beard matted with soap, and brandishing a long open cut-throat razor.

With a whoop of terror the slaves dropped everything they were handling, and leaped out of the window. And before the Sultan could say 'Bismillahi!' (in the name of Allah!), the apparition pounced upon him dragging him clear out of the tub right across the bathroom floor and straight through the open doorway.

The next instant the roof of the bathroom caved in with a shattering crash, bringing the four walls down with it in a heap of rubble and broken beams and rafters.

'My saviour! My brother!' shouted the Sultan. 'Thou hast saved my life. . . . Thou hast snatched me out of the very jaws of death. . . . How can I ever repay thee. . . .'

And to the shouting jostling crowd who pressed around from every corner of the building, wondering, asking questions, the Sultan recounted his miraculous escape from death, and how this, his own incomparable adviser and seer had foreseen it all and had rushed to his rescue, not a second too soon.

A murmur of awe and admiration ran through the crowd. But in the midst of it all Sheikh Ramadan stood sorrowfully silent. Fool, fool, that he was! He had tried to run away from Destiny. But Destiny had forestalled him and turned against him the very trick he had employed to escape her. Fool, triple fool! Did he really think he could run away from the *maktoob,* or modify it in any way? Again, Destiny's voice rang in his ears: '*Maktoob,* O Son of Adam. It is all *maktoob,* and from the *maktoob* there is no escape.'

Patiently he waited for the tumult around him to subside. Then he quietly retired to his rooms, and there in abstinence and prayer, sought pardon and forgiveness for his foolish presumptuousness.

And so, once again the years came and went, bringing more and more fulfilment to Sheikh Ramadan.

Then, one day, a neighbouring Prince came to ask for the hand of the Sultan's daughter in marriage. The Sultan sought the counsel of his now well established adviser and seer, and Sheikh Ramadan in his turn consulted the oracles and declared the answer extremely favourable.

This caused great rejoicing in the Palace for the prospective bridegroom was one of the richest and handsomest princes in the land, and the Sultan couldn't have wished a better alliance for his daughter. He therefore decided to make this the most memorable wedding of the year, and had towncriers sent throughout the land to proclaim the happy event, and special couriers despatched to all neighbouring Emirs and Princes with a personal invitation for the wedding of his daughter.

So, after the customary forty days and nights of great festivities, the wedding day dawned, serene and bright, to the gay sound of drums and cymbals, and the plaintive tune of flutes and *rabab.*

The Sultan, beaming with happiness, stood welcoming his guests under a great marquee which was erected in the midst of the Royal Gardens for the occasion, and facing this marquee a roomy dais with a trellis of jasmine and roses was erected for the Sultana and her ladies-in-waiting.

Destiny

Sheikh Ramadan stood close to the Sultan who now treated him like a brother, and shared fully in the congratulations for the wedding. This was to be a red-letter day in his life, for he knew that every royal guest had come with a question to put to him. Normally this would not have troubled him, for his fame as an adviser and seer had now long since been established. But today, for some inexplicable reason, his spirit was vaguely disturbed, and he felt unsure of himself and strangely restless.

In the meantime dancers and jesters kept the royal assembly amused, and the eating and drinking continued far into the late afternoon.

Then, as the sun began to dip behind the Palace walls, one of the Emirs stepped briskly out into the royal gardens, and returned shortly thereafter. He then went up to Sheikh Ramadan, and holding out to him a closed fist, asked him pointedly if he could guess what it was he held in there.

Sheikh Ramadan's restlessness had considerably increased. He couldn't shake it off. And though he sought desperately for inspiration, it wouldn't come. Was he going to disgrace himself today of all days in the presence of this assembled royalty?

Pity for his sorry plight seized him. And comparing himself in his present predicament to something as insignificant as a grasshopper, he murmured sadly:

'You poor wretched grasshopper! The first time you managed to escape;' (he was alluding here to his discovery of the Sultan's safe), 'and the second time you also managed to escape;' (and here he was alluding to the collapse of the Sultan's bathroom), 'but the third time, you poor wretched grasshopper, methinks, you have fallen into the Emir's clutches!'

'By Allah!' cried the Emir, opening his hand and letting a fat grasshopper drop out of it. 'Thou art indeed the greatest seer of this age, for twice have I attempted to catch this grasshopper, and twice it had eluded me!'

Great cheers and loud clapping of hands followed. And the most exuberant in his praise was the Sultan who strutted proudly round, saying: 'What did I tell you!'

Now a second Emir, who was old and frail, expressed a wish to put a question to Sheikh Ramadan. And in deference to the Emir's age and state of health, Sheikh Ramadan rose to go over to him. He had now fully recovered his equanimity and self assurance, and felt ready to answer any question.

But hardly had he taken a couple of steps forward than he stood transfixed. Destiny was there, right before him: ruthless and resplendent in her shimmering robes and riding high on her great glimmering ball of white cloud, as she smilingly waved him good-bye.

Sheikh Ramadan couldn't take his eyes off her. His stiff lips moved in a silent prayer of entreaty for her to remain with him just a little while longer; and unconsciously he clasped his hands and lifted them up to her in a gesture of strong appeal.

Every princely head in the assembly turned to follow his gaze. All they could see was the Sultana who had risen in her dais as if wishing to depart.

A low murmur of astonishment went round. And the Sultan's face was suddenly dark with hatred and fury.

'By Allah!' he cried, drawing out his bejewelled dagger. 'The dog dares to lift his eyes to my wife in public, and for this insult he shall pay with his life in public.'

So saying, he plunged his dagger deep into the heart of the hapless Sheikh who sank to his knees in a pool of blood, murmuring: 'Destiny! Treacherous Destiny! Who can ever escape thee. . . .'

The Sultan and the Cobbler

There was once a Sultan and he liked to walk through the streets of his kingdom, from time to time, and stop to chat unceremoniously with the rank and file he met on the way, and the traders and cattledealers who crowded the market-place.

He thus hoped to find out for himself how loyal his people were to his throne, and how contented or otherwise they were with his rule. But the people, warned beforehand by the Vizier never to importune His Majesty with their troubles and tribulations, would always show a happy face to the Sultan and never fail to assure him of their gratitude for his bounty and their allegiance to his throne.

Then, one day, the Sultan decided to walk incognito through the streets of his kingdom, unaccompanied by the Vizier or any other member of his royal retinue. The Vizier tried hard to dissuade him from so doing, pointing out the dangers which could ensue to the personal safety of the Sultan from such an adventure. But the Sultan remained unmoved. 'If my people are as content with my rule as they appear to be, and as loyal to my throne as they profess to be,' he argued, 'then I see no reason to fear for my personal safety.'

So, soon after the dusk of night had fallen, the Sultan threw a long dark cloak over his shoulders, and pulling the hood well over his head, slipped quietly out of the palace into the streets of his kingdom.

It was not long before he found himself in the busy centre of town, and was roughly hustled and jostled by the passers-by, some of whom barely deigned to return his polite greetings. Nonetheless, he walked on, keeping his eyes and ears wide open to everything which was said and done around him.

He, however, carefully avoided the crowded cafés and drinking places for fear of being detected at close quarters, and sought instead the friendly darkness of a back alley, or a deserted doorway, where he could stand and listen undisturbed to the many scraps of conversation which reached him through the open windows of the brightly-lit homes of the well-to-do.

But there was neither merriment nor contentment in the voices that reached him. Some groused and grumbled; some bemoaned their financial losses or their bad digestions; some threatened to divorce their wives or break off with their business partners; and some cursed Iblees and the high taxes. But not a word of praise or gratitude for the Sultan, and not a joke or laugh or song anywhere.

'Faith!' thought the Sultan. 'A more despondent lot cannot exist!'

Disgruntled, he then turned his footsteps in the direction of the poorer part of town, picking his way through a maze of narrow, pitted, dusty lanes by the flicker of a candle light shining through the small narrow openings that stood for windows in the mud wall of some humble homes, or by the brighter light of a kerosene lamp swinging over a gaping doorway.

But here again he was struck by the absence of all indication of joy or merriment in the scraps of conversation which reached him, and he began to wonder if all the crowds that met him on his customary walks with such a show of warmheartedness and contentment were indeed his own people and part of his own kingdom.

Feeling now thoroughly depressed and dejected, he began to retrace his footsteps, when the sound of merry singing suddenly filled the night air.

'By Allah!' thought the Sultan, instantly perking up. 'Here at last is someone with the true joy of living in his heart.' And hurriedly he walked in the direction of the singing voice.

Presently he came to a humble abode, and peering through a small opening in the mud wall, he saw a young man of pleasant appearance sitting on a strip of matting and singing away to his heart's content as he stitched diligently at a pair of leather soles.

'A cobbler,' mused the Sultan as his eyes wandered lazily round the small bare room, 'and a pretty poor one at that! Yet there he is, as merry as a lord, and as I live I must discover the secret of his happiness.'

With that, he pulled the hood of his cloak further over his head, and simulating a weary old man, stepped uncertainly over the threshold.

'Greetings, son!' he said in a tremulous voice. 'I seem to have lost my way in the dark, and would fain solicit a drink of water and a few minutes respite to rest my weary limbs.'

The young man sprang up to meet him. 'Marhaba Yaba!' (Welcome, old father), he said, as he helped the Sultan across the room and eased him on to a strip of matting next to which stood a *tabliya* (a low wooden circular table), bearing a chunk of bread and a water *gulla* (jar). 'There now! Rest yourself for as long as you wish, and here is water to slake your thirst and bread to restore your strength.' He then pushed the chunk of bread and the water *gulla* across the *tabliya* towards the Sultan, and went back to resume his work.

The Sultan took a good pull from the water *gulla,* and gratefully stretched his aching legs. Then, after a decent pause, he broke off a piece of bread and said as he chewed upon it painfully: 'Tell me, son. You seem, Allah be praised, a very contented mortal. Is yours a lucrative trade?'

'I find it so,' said the young man cheerfully. 'It brings me in four piastres a day, and for that I am truly thankful.'

'Four piastres!' said the Sultan, unable to keep the surprise out of his voice. 'And can you manage to meet all your requirements on four piastres a day?'

'Easily,' returned the young man. 'I eat one piastre, I repay the second, I lend the third, and I throw the fourth into the river.'

The Sultan mulled this over for a while and then said: 'You talk in riddles, son, I cannot follow you.'

'Then I will explain,' said the young man good-humouredly. 'The piastre I eat is the one I spend on my food; the piastre I repay is the one I give to my father for having looked after me; the piastre I lend is the one I spend on my sons who, in turn, will one day look after me; and the piastre I throw into the river is the one I spend on my daughters from whom I do not expect any repayment since they will have to leave me one day and follow their husbands.'

The Sultan was so delighted with this novel explanation, that he threw caution to the four winds and openly declared himself to the cobbler.

'Here is a thousand rials,' he said, tossing a bagful across to him. 'But until you have seen my face a thousand times, I forbid you to repeat to any living soul what you have just told me.'

With that, he walked briskly out of the cobbler's presence, chuckling to himself as he disappeared in the darkness of night: 'What a quiz for the wise old men of my kingdom!'

Early next morning he convened Court and said to his councillors: 'I have a riddle for you, my learned friends. A man earns four piastres a day; he eats one; he repays one; he lends one, and he throws one into the river. Now, how in fact does he apportion his earnings?'

The councillors looked at him and then at each other with blank faces. They then begged for time to consult and debate together. The Sultan granted them three full

days, but when on the morning of the fourth day they still had no answer forthcoming, he flew into a temper and threatened to have them all disgraced and thrown into jail.

The Vizier, who was to share in the punishment, panicked. What to do? Who to turn to? Suddenly a thought struck him: The Sultan had come out with this riddle the morning after the night he had spent on his own in the streets of the kingdom. 'Therefore,' decided the Vizier, 'it is in the streets of the kingdom, and not here in the royal palace, that the answer to the riddle is to be found.'

So, as soon as he had seen his liege safely to bed that night, the Vizier stole out of the palace and walked through one street after the other, in the residential part of town, taking careful note of any word or deed which could throw some light on the riddle he had set out to solve. But in vain.

Dismayed, he turned towards the poorer quarter of town, and after tripping and stumbling into many a dirty dusty pit, the sound of merry singing suddenly fell on his ears.

'Allah be praised!' thought the Vizier, his spirits rising. 'This is indeed a presage of good hope.' And guided by the singing voice which seemed to jollify the dark night, he presently came to the cobbler's humble home, and boldly stepped across the threshold.

'Greetings, friend,' he said. 'You sound so happy and contented that I would fain spend a few minutes in your company to dispel my own gloom.'

'Marhaba,' said the young man rising to meet him. 'And what, Allah forbid, may your trouble be?'

The Vizier then spoke to him of the riddle the Sultan had posed to his councillors, and of his threat to have them disgraced and thrown into jail if they failed to come with the correct answer by morning. 'But what *can* the correct answer be,' pursued the Vizier anxiously.

'I am ready to pay a thousand rials to anyone who can come forward with it.'

The cobbler was silent for a long while, then he said: 'I can give you the correct answer; on condition that you do not tell the Sultan I have spoken.'

The Vizier readily agreed. He paid the cobbler a thousand rials, and returned to the palace jubilantly hugging to his heart the correct answer to the riddle.

Next day, still secretly chuckling over the discomfiture of his councillors, the Sultan convened Court. But great was his surprise when the spokesman for the councillors rose and delivered before the assembly the correct answer to the riddle.

At that, the Sultan's suspicion was instantly roused. 'So the cobbler has blabbed,' he shouted angrily. 'Get the son-of-a-bitch here, at once. . . . I will have him impaled on the highest minaret for disobeying my orders.'

The Vizier tried hard to intercede for the hapless cobbler. But the Sultan remained unrelenting.

In due course the cobbler was hustled to the palace, and stood serene and unruffled before the throne.

'Now, dog!' roared the Sultan. 'What have you to say for yourself? Have I not forbidden you to speak until you have seen my face a thousand times?'

'That is so, my Liege,' said the cobbler calmly. 'But before I spoke I had not only seen your face one thousand times, but two thousand times.'

With that, he shook out of a small bag he was carrying, two thousand rials each of which bore the effigy of the Sultan's head.

Once again, the Sultan was so delighted with the cobbler's answer, that he not only dismissed him with full pardon, but also gave him another bagful of one thousand rials.

Different times have different 'adans'

There was once a Sultan and he was strolling through his lands one day, when he saw a fellah digging away so assiduously at a small patch of land, that he was unaware of a snake which had crept up to him and started coiling itself round his ankle.

Alarmed, the Sultan shouted a warning. But the fellah merely shook off the snake and, without even attempting to kill it, went calmly on with his digging.

The Sultan was frankly amazed at the fellah's unconcern. 'Man!' he said to him. 'Don't you realize that that snake could have killed you? Yet all you do is to shake it off as if it didn't matter, and calmly go on with your digging!'

'Your Majesty,' said the fellah, 'I face death every day of my life; not from a snake, but from this very patch of land you see me digging. For if I do not put into it every ounce of strength I possess, I run the risk of starving to death since what it produces is hardly sufficient for mine and my children's bare subsistence.'

The Sultan was so moved by the fellah's wretched circumstances, that he ordered his Vizier to give him a substantial grant to help him out.

Months later, the Sultan was again strolling through his lands when he perceived the same fellah. This time, however, he was not digging. And though he wore his right arm in a sling, he was well dressed and looked fat and prosperous.

Curious to know how he now fared, the Sultan stopped to talk to him. 'And what is the matter with your arm, my man?' he asked.

'Your Majesty,' replied the fellah, 'last night I pricked

my finger on a cucumber thorn, so I thought I would rest my arm this morning.'

'Subhan Allah!' (Glory be to God), said the Sultan in wonderment. 'When you were poor and destitute you weren't mindful of a snake which could have killed you outright. Now that you are fat and prosperous, a cucumber thorn can put you right out of action?'

'O Sultan!' said the fellah unabashed. 'Let us not forget that different times have different *adans*.' (The *adan* is the man who calls the faithful to prayer).

'O luck of the ugly . . .'

In the days of long ago, there once lived a peasant who had several sons of whom he was very proud. For they were all hearty and strong and helped him till the land and harvest the crop, and thus gave him a lot of joy in life. But in this joy the peasant's wife did not fully share, for she wanted a daughter.

'Sons are all very well to share in their father's labour,' she would say, 'but who's to stand by a mother's death-bed in her old age and close her eyes and compose her limbs, if not a daughter?'

So, having heard of a newly arrived magician in the district, she went secretly to consult him one night. 'I will give you a hundred rials and the first calf of the season if you can make me have a daughter,' she said to him.

The magician asked for her name and her mother's name, then he brought out a large china dish on the borders of which he drew several exotic designs over which he recited a long string of incantations. He then washed off the designs with a little water which he bottled up and handed over to the peasant's wife.

'Wait until the new moon is born,' he said to her, then

wash yourself with some of this water every night for seven nights running, and Allah willing, you will have a daughter.'

The peasant's wife thanked him, and when the new moon was born, did exactly as he had told her. In due course she became pregnant, and this time she gave birth to a daughter.

There was great rejoicing over the event, and friends and relations came from far and near to say *'Mabrook'* (congratulations), and share in the celebrations. The peasant's wife fasted and prayed and invoked all the good spirits in Heaven above and on the earth beneath, to preside over her daughter's happiness and protect her from all evil. The peasant, too, fasted and prayed and gave alms to the poor in thanksgiving to Almighty Allah for having blessed him with a daughter.

And so, pampered, cherished and indulged, the daughter thrived and grew. But the older she grew, the uglier she became. So ugly was she in fact, that her parents, fearing lest she be shocked at the sight of her own reflection, strictly forbade the use of any mirror in their home.

Yet, ugly though she was, the girl had a sweet nature which won her many friends and endeared her to all those who came in contact with her. Nonetheless, when she became of marriageable age, no young man came forward to ask for her hand in marriage. And the parents began to have great qualms as to who would ever want to marry their ugly daughter, when there were so many beautiful girls around.

The mother paid several secret visits to every renowned magician in the district, and the peasant seized every opportunity to make it widely known that he intended to make a handsome settlement on his daughter the day of her wedding. But the seasons followed fast one on to the other, and still no suitor came forward.

Then, one day, much to everybody's surprise, the girl's own cousin – a rich handsome young man on whom the heart of all the eligible young maidens in the district was set, came to ask for her hand in marriage. The parents' joy was unbounded. And the girl was in the seventh heaven of delight, for she loved her cousin dearly and had secretly hoped he would ask her to marry him.

So, festivities for the wedding commenced forty days in advance, and once again, friends and relations came from far and near to say *'Mabrook'* and share in the celebrations. But though they were all outwardly lavish in their praise and good wishes for the promised couple, inwardly they were all green with envy and went away wondering what could have induced such a handsome young man to choose such an ugly girl for a bride when there were so many beautiful ones around?

The girl herself was totally oblivious to the talk and stir her engagement to her cousin had created. For was it not the normal custom for a man to look for a bride amongst his own kinsfolk before starting to look for one amongst strangers?

She, therefore, responded to all the praise and good wishes which were showered upon her, with proud open joy, and not a trace of humility or gratitude for what others regarded as her 'great good luck'.

There was one person, however, who found it very hard to reconcile herself to this so-called 'great good luck' of the peasant's ugly daughter. And that was her best friend – a rich and beautiful maiden who was very much in love with the prospective bridegroom and had been hoping all along that he would ask her to marry him.

When she heard that he had taken his suit to his ugly cousin, she laughed derisively, and said: 'Wait until he's seen her face . . . he'll then soon recover his senses. . . .'

But, as the wedding day drew nearer and nearer, and she finally realized that she had irrevocably lost the man she loved to her ugly rival, hatred and envy so filled her heart that she could neither eat nor sleep.

Then, early one morning she went to visit the peasant's daughter. And after a few polite preliminaries, said to her bluntly: 'Tell me, my dear, have you ever seen your reflection in a mirror?'

The girl looked at her in candid surprise. 'No,' she answered mildly, 'now that you mention it, I don't think I have.'

'Then you should,' said her friend brutally, and forthwith took her leave.

As soon as her friend had departed, the girl went to her mother and asked for a mirror to see her face. The mother became alarmed, and tried hard to argue her daughter out of the subject. But the more she argued, the more was the girl determined to see her reflection.

So, having failed to find a mirror at home, or get her mother to buy or borrow one for her, she waited until the sun had set and the household had retired, then stole quietly out of the house and made straight for the river.

The moon was resplendent in its fourteenth night, the air was still, and the face of the river shone like a polished mirror. Gently, the girl waded in, and bending over, saw for the first time in her life, the reflection of her face in the waters of the river.

She was so appalled at her ugliness, that she decided then and there to do away with her life. 'But not here . . . not in the river . . .' she sobbed broken-heartedly, 'not where my body would be recovered and people would gather round to gloat and commiserate over my ugliness.'

She decided instead to get lost in the wilderness where some wild beast of prey would be sure to devour her and so efface forever all trace of her existence.

She hadn't walked far when a tall handsome stranger

suddenly appeared before her. Alarmed, the girl drew her veil closer to her face and averted her head in the hope that the stranger would proceed on his way. But he didn't. He came up to her, and putting a light hand on her shoulder, said gently: 'Where are you going all alone at this time of night?'

His touch was so gentle and his voice so reassuring, that the girl broke down and confided to him her trouble. 'My cousin is a gallant young man,' she concluded tearfully. 'I now realize that he has asked me to marry him only because he knew that no other man ever will. I am so ugly . . . and he is so young and handsome and desirable. . . . But the sacrifice is too great . . . I cannot accept it . . . I must set him free.'

'Look at me,' the stranger interposed quietly, 'am I not as young and handsome and desirable as your cousin?'

Shyly and timidly the girl's eyes rested upon him. 'Indeed you are, Sir.'

'Well then, that's how you appear in the eyes of your cousin: young, handsome and desirable, for I am your luck. . . . I stand up for you all the time. So go back home and have no more qualms about your looks. Looks don't matter. . . . It's luck that matters. . . .'

With that he vanished into the night.

Utterly bewildered, but with greatly uplifted spirits, the girl returned home, and quietly re-entered her room. Nobody had had time to miss her.

In due course she and her cousin got married and lived happily together ever after.

Hence the popular Sudanese saying:

> 'Ya bakht ash-sheina,
> Agif leina.'

> 'O luck of the Ugly,
> Stand up for us.'

The man who did not believe in luck

'When luck decides to leave you, the strongest chains cannot hold it back; and when luck decides to come to you, a single hair can lead it along.' Thus spoke the wise elders of a town in which there once lived a man who did not believe in luck.

He started business as a small retailer of sorts. Then, luck favoured him, and year after year his profits increased and his business expanded until he finally became one of the richest and most important merchants of his town.

'How lucky you are!' those who like him had started small, but had failed to attain the same standard of success, would say to him. To which he would boastfully reply: 'There is no such thing as luck. My success is due entirely to my own ability.'

And so, the years came and went, and our merchant became richer and richer. Then, one day, he decided to move to a neighbouring town where he thought his business prospects would be even greater. And not wishing to encumber himself with a load of bulky merchandise, he converted all his assets into precious stones and nuggets of pure gold.

These he packed into a couple of saddlebags, and after saying good-bye to all his friends and relations, he mounted his horse and set forth bright and early one morning to his new destination.

By noon he came to a clump of shady trees that stood on the edge of a cool clear stream. And as the day was hot and dusty, the merchant couldn't have wished for a more ideal spot in which to break his journey and enjoy a short rest.

The man who did not believe in luck

So, he dismounted. And without bothering to remove his saddlebags, he led the horse to the water. Then he kicked off his *markoob* (footwear), and cast off his caftan, and wading into the stream drank deep and long of the cool clear water and liberally soused his head and face.

Feeling thus rested and refreshed, he sat enjoying a leisurely smoke in the shade of the trees, when suddenly he noticed that his horse's legs were fast sinking into the stream.

Up he leapt in alarm and rushed to the horse tugging and pulling wildly at its bridle in an attempt to lead it out of the water. But the harder he pulled and tugged, the deeper the horse sank until finally it disappeared into the stream, saddlebags and all.

Distraught, the merchant beat his chest and tore his hair and loudly lamented his misfortune: 'Woe, woe! I am a ruined man. . . . My riches. . . . My entire fortune. . . . My whole life's labour. . . . All gone. . . . Vanished for ever. . . ! What will I do. . . ? Where will I go. . . ?

For a long time he sat thus by the water edge filling the air with his lamentations. Finally he rose, undecided whether to proceed to his new destination, or return to his old home town. But rather than return to his old home town, ruined and destitute as he now was, he decided to proceed to his new destination where, he felt confident, a man of his repute would have no difficulty in finding someone willing enough to advance him a substantial sum of money that would tide him over his present dilemma.

To his chagrin and disappointment, however, when he did arrive at his new destination, he soon discovered that though his successful business reputation had indeed preceded him, not one of all the important business people he went to see was willing to advance him the smallest sum of money, or offer him the smallest chance of earning a day's living. All they had to offer was their sympathy and commiseration in his bad luck, and their wishes for better luck in the future.

And so, day followed day, bringing no success despite the most valiant efforts the merchant deployed in his search for work. Any work.

In the end, when the situation became desperate, he reluctantly came to the conclusion that to remain where he was would be pointless. He therefore decided to return to his old home town. For there, at least, his town folk knew him, and even if he failed to raise a loan, some of the less successful business people would, he felt sure, have no hesitation in engaging him and so benefit by his experience and his outstanding business abilities.

Accordingly, at break of dawn one morning, he set out on his return journey home, and by late afternoon he reached the same shady spot alongside the running stream into which his horse had disappeared.

Sore-footed and weary he sat by the water edge, silently grieving over the loss of his riches, and wondering if, after all, there was such a thing as luck – good and bad? For, if indeed he owed his business success to good luck, then he must equally attribute the misfortune which had befallen him, to bad luck. Otherwise, how else could he account for his negligence in not thinking of removing the saddlebags before leading his horse to the water?

If, therefore, there *was* such a thing as luck – good and bad, then, 'O Allah, for a stroke of good luck to restore to me my lost riches,' was his earnest prayer.

With that he rose, kicked off his *markoob* and cast off his caftan, then wading well into the stream, he scooped up some water and bent his head to drink from his cupped hands. But there was a hair floating therein. So he threw that water away and scooped up a fresh lot. But there again was the hair.

The merchant was greatly intrigued. He took a firm hold of the hair, between thumb and forefinger, and smartly pulled it out of his hand. Then he tried to flick it off, but the hair remained stuck to his fingers, and as he kept drawing at it, it seemed to have no end and grew longer and longer in his hand.

The merchant's curiosity was now fully roused. What *was* this hair that persisted in sticking to his hand and seemed to come from the bottom of the stream?

Carefully, so as not to break it, he kept drawing at it and the hair kept getting longer and longer. In a few moments a second hair appeared alongside the first, then a third and a fourth; then a half dozen and a dozen, and soon what looked like the bushy tail of a horse broke through the surface of the stream.

Wild with excitement, the merchant grabbed the tail with both hands and pulled and heaved. Presently the rump of a horse came into view, then the flanks, then the neck and head, and finally the legs. O joy! It was his own lost horse, and, miracle of miracles. . . ! With saddlebags intact!

'Allah! How lucky I am,' shouted the merchant aloud. And from that day on, knew better than to say, 'There is no such thing as luck.'

The poor man's bowl

There was once a poor man and he was honest and simple and quite content with his lowly lot. At the end of each day he would thank Almighty Allah for the few piastres he was able to earn, and after supper he would sit with his wife and children on the doorstep of their humble home, and together they would laugh and sing and tell each other tales of miraculous happenings and heroic adventures.

The poor man's bowl

Now not very far from where this poor man lived, there was a rich man and he had a truly palatial home. It was expensively furnished and well lit every night, but no sound of song or laughter ever came from it. For the rich man always groused and grumbled and, in consequence, his wife and children always shunned him.

So, left to himself, he would sit and brood gloomily by his open window, and as he thus sat, night after night, he couldn't help noticing how happy, by contrast, was the poor man with *his* wife and children.

Soon envy began to corrode his heart. And like all envious people, he could find no peace until he had wrecked the poor man's happiness. But how? The quickest and surest way would be to deprive him of his daily bread, for one cannot sing and laugh on an empty stomach.

Accordingly, he went one morning to the pottery-yard where the poor man was employed, and asked his employer to dismiss him. 'He and his family are a rowdy lot,' he said to him, 'they shout and quarrel every night and disturb my peace.' And because he was a man of substance, the employer readily gratified his wish. He dismissed the poor man, and that night no sound of song or laughter issued from the humble mud-hut. The rich man took good note of this, and went to bed gloating.

In the days that followed, the poor man did all he could to find himself a job of work. But he failed. Soon, his meagre savings had dwindled, and one morning his wife said to him: 'This is the last piastre we have in the house. Take it and go and buy some *fool* (a popular native dish of cooked beans) for the children. After that, Allah will have to provide.'

The poor man picked up a chipped wooden bowl and went to buy the *fool*. On his way back he tripped and fell, spilling the whole bowlful of *fool* on the ground.

The poor man's bowl

Ruefully he surveyed the mess at his feet. It would be pointless for him to go back home now empty-handed to his wife and children. But he would save the bowl. It could come in useful, some time or other.

So, he cleaned it out with a handful of dry earth, and clapped it on his head for want of a more convenient place in which to keep it. He then walked to the river in the hope of finding himself a job of work for the day.

As he reached the river he saw a boat with several men aboard, ready to set out. He asked the mate if he needed an extra pair of hands, and the mate who was in fact short of man-power, took him on.

After a few hours, when the boat was right out in the middle of the river, a fierce storm broke out, and the boat was wrecked on an island inhabited by a primitive tribe. Some of the men were drowned, and some, amongst them the poor man, were able to swim to the island for safety.

As soon as the men scrambled ashore, the islanders surrounded them and led them on to their Chief who was sitting cooling himself from the hot midday sun under a large awning of reeds. He looked suspiciously at the men lined up before him, and his eyes immediately fastened on the poor man who stood conspicuously out from the rest by the wooden bowl he wore on his head.

'What brings you to my island?' he asked him gruffly.

'Fate!' replied the poor man simply.

'And what is this curious device you wear on your head?'

'A wooden bowl,' said the poor man, taking it off and handing it over to the Chief.

The Chief, who had never seen a wooden bowl before, turned it curiously round and round in his hand. 'And why do you wear it on your head?'

'As a protection from the sun,' replied the poor man on impulse.

The Chief grunted, but was not entirely reassured. So

he clapped the wooden bowl on his head and took a few turns in the hot midday sun. His head felt decidedly cooler.

'I want this bowl,' he said to the poor man as he resumed his seat under the reed awning, 'and in return I will give you anything you like from this island.'

'I would just like to return home to my wife and children,' said the poor man.

'I will see to that,' said the Chief. 'But since I have taken something from you, I cannot let you go back empty-handed.'

With that, he dipped his hand into a reed basket next to him, and scooped out of it handful after handful of rubies, turquoise and emeralds. 'You can amuse your children with these sparkling bits of glass,' he said, as he threw these magnificent gems into the biggest lap the poor man could make out of his tattered *gallabiya*. He then instructed his men to escort the poor man safely to the water-front where he hailed a passing boat which took him across.

As soon as he landed he went straight to market and bought all the victuals he could carry home to his wife and children. And that night, after a truly festive supper, the sound of song and laughter once again issued from his humble mud-hut.

The rich man heard it. But assuming it was just a break resulting from some temporary menial job the poor man might have finally succeeded in finding, went to bed little perturbed.

When, however, the sound of rejoicing continued to reach him, night after night, the green snake of envy once again stirred in his breast. So, feigning the sincerity and concern of one good neighbour for the other, he went across to the poor man one evening, and asked him what could have caused such a happy change in his hitherto tragic circumstances.

And the poor man, being the honest simple fellow

that he was, with no malice in his heart, and not suspecting for a moment that his rich neighbour was the sole cause of all his earlier trouble, told him the full story of his adventure. 'But now,' he concluded gratefully, 'Allah be praised! For neither my family nor I need ever go hungry again.'

The rich man listened to this story in stony silence. And his heart well nigh burst with greed and envy. He returned to his home and sat brooding gloomily all night by his open window. At daybreak an idea suddenly occurred to him: Why shouldn't he too make the journey to the island? 'For,' he cunningly deliberated, 'if the Chief thought it fit to give the poor man all those precious stones for a mere chipped wooden bowl, how much more is he not likely to give *me* for all the handsome gifts I would take to him?'

So, as soon as his household was astir that morning, he ordered dozens of turkeys and geese and pigeons to be killed and plucked and roasted, and when he had packed these into several reed baskets, he filled several other baskets with butter and eggs and hot loaves and fresh cheese, and then hired a boat which took him and his gifts across to the island.

It was noontime. And as soon as he landed the tribesmen surrounded him and led him on to their Chief who sat cooling himself under the reed awning.

'What brings you to my island?' the Chief asked him gruffly.

'A burning desire to see you and greet you,' smirked the rich man, bowing and scraping in humble affection.

'And what have you in all these baskets?' said the Chief eyeing them suspiciously.

'Just a few humble gifts, which please deign to accept,' said the rich man ingratiatingly. And without waiting to be asked, he started opening one basket after the other, and placing it before the Chief.

The Chief dipped his hand into each basket in turn,

sampling the contents with great gusto, and grunting his appreciation and contentment as he went along.

He then distributed the rest of the food amongst the tribe who sat gathered around him. And when they too had expressed their appreciation and contentment, munching and crunching their way through the entire contents of the baskets, the Chief turned to the rich man who stood hopefully by, and said to him:

'As you see, your gifts were most welcome. And to prove to you how greatly I have appreciated them, I am now going to give you the most precious object I have in this island.'

So saying, he drew out of a reed basket next to him, the poor man's chipped wooden bowl, and handed it ceremoniously over to the rich man.

A discerning old 'faki'

There was once a woman and she was young and pretty. But she led an unhappy life with her husband who constantly beat and abused her, for she was tactless and domineering and never had an endearing word to say to him.

One day when she felt she could take her husband's ill-treatment no longer, she went to see a wise old *faki*, and asked him to prepare her a *hegab* (a charm) which would make her husband love her.

'Willingly,' said the old *faki*, after listening to her story attentively, 'but for the *hegab* to be efficacious, I would require two hairs out of a live lion's whiskers.'

'Is that all?' queried the woman, showing little concern about the magnitude of the request.

'That is all,' said the wise old *faki*.

'You shall have the two hairs this very night,' said the woman, and promptly took her leave.

From there she went to market where she bought a fat young lamb and took it home. Then, when the sun began to set, she slung a goatskin of water across her shoulder, and leading the lamb on a short length of rope behind her, stole quietly out of the house and walked swiftly in the direction of the wilderness where an old lion had his den.

By the faint light of a half moon she then dug a hole wherein she emptied her water-skin, and when she had tied the lamb to a stake near the water-hole, she hid behind a thornbush and there, still as a mouse, sat and waited.

Presently the lamb shivered and began to bleat. The lion heard it and came out of his den growling and sniffing the air. Soon he caught the lamb's scent and sprang upon it. When he had quite devoured it, he drank deep of the water in the hole and thus, content and replete, began to sway drowsily on his feet.

At that moment, the woman who was following the whole scene very closely from behind her thornbush, sprang noiselessly out of her hiding place, in time to pillow the lion's head on her lap, as he sank heavily to the ground in deep torpor.

Softly, she then started crooning to him, and gently she stroked his head, working her fingers lightly further and further down his face. In a few moments he began to snore. And judging that he was now too far gone in sleep to feel any disturbance, the woman singled out two hairs in his whiskers, and smartly pulled them out.

The lion stirred and growled. The woman increased her crooning and caressing, and soon had him soothed back to peaceful slumber. She then gently slipped his head off her lap, and ran off to the *faki* with her precious trophy.

'Here you are!' she said, holding the two hairs coolly out to him. 'And now tell me, how soon can I have my *hegab*?'

The wise old *faki* contemplated her for a few minutes in silence. Then he said: 'If you could manage to pull two hairs out of a live lion's whiskers, you do not need the intervention of a *hegab* to make your husband love you.'

The old crone who was more wily than Iblees

Iblees, the Devil, was one morning sitting in the corner of a road, silently contemplating a busy silkshop opposite, when an old crone came stumping by and asked him why he looked so pensive.

'Well,' said Iblees, 'I was just thinking: I have succeeded in sowing discord amongst friends of long standing in this community, and I have equally succeeded in breaking up many a happy home. But try as I will I cannot succeed in destroying the happiness of that shopkeeper yonder. For he and his wife are as close together today, as when they first married; and that is already several moons past.'

'Huh!' grunted the old crone. 'As likely as not, you've lost your wiles.'

'I have, have I?' scoffed Iblees. 'Then mayhap *you* can show me how to set about it.'

'And right gladly too!' was the tart rejoinder. 'Come this way again tonight, and see for yourself how brilliantly I shall have succeeded where you have so sadly failed.'

And without giving Iblees a chance to say another word, the old crone turned her back squarely upon him and stumped off to her home.

Once there, she started transforming herself from a

eric fraser

withered bedraggled old hag, into a respectable old lady of the affluent society. First of all, she gave herself a thoroughly good scrubbing, and when she had carefully made up her face and neck, to dissimulate as much as possible the coarse roughness of her leathery skin, she sprayed herself with a fragrant scent, and then stepped into an elegant attire which drew many an appreciative glance to her as she crossed the road and walked sedately into the busy silkshop opposite.

The shopkeeper perceived her, and scenting a customer of class, hastened forward, all smiles and bows, ready to serve her.

Courteously he led her to the plush-covered settee he usually reserved for customers of her standing, and when she had graciously accepted the lighted cigarette he offered her, she sat languidly back and asked to be shown the costliest silks in the shop.

'Certainly, Madam!' said the shopkeeper, as he hastened to pull off the shelves several rolls of his finest silks and display them before her.

The old lady surveyed the variety of kaleidoscopic colours with a critical eye. She then picked out a couple of exotic designs, and as she seemed undecided which of the two to choose, she frankly appealed to the shopkeeper to help her make up her mind.

The shopkeeper was only too ready to oblige. But, was it for a young person, or for someone of more mature age?

The old lady laughed shortly. 'In other words, is it for me, or for a younger member of my family? Well, to tell you the truth, it is for a complete stranger. In fact, it is for a married woman, with whom my son, much to my distress, is hopelessly in love; nonetheless, he asked me to choose it for her.'

She paused for a while to let this information sink in; then, raising sorrowful eyes to the shopkeeper's face, she proceeded with a sad little sigh: 'Can you think what a heartbreak it is for me to see my son – my only son, fritter away his youth and his money on a married woman, when he could have easily found himself a wife from amongst the best families in the land, and so made my happiness in my old age?'

The shopkeeper was all sympathy and understanding, and had many words of comfort to offer. In the end, he succeeded in helping the old lady make up her mind, and proceeded to cut the required length of silk. He then folded it up, and as he turned slightly round to reach for a sheet of wrapping paper, the old lady surreptitiously held her lighted cigarette close to the edge of the material, thus burning a hole through several folds in it.

Then, with a show of great dismay, she tried to snuff the fire out, apologizing profusely the while for her unpardonable carelessness, and attributing it to the unhappy state of her mind over her son's unfortunate entanglement with a married woman.

The shopkeeper couldn't but redouble his expression of sympathy and understanding, and gallantly offered to replace the length of silk for her. But the old lady insisted on keeping it, pointing out that as the burnt parts were luckily all close up to the selvedge, a clever dressmaker would have no difficulty in dissimulating them when cutting out the material.

The shopkeeper saw her point. So he wrapped up the silk, and the old lady left the shop carrying her parcel well hidden under her shawl.

A little way further up the road, she stopped and knocked at a door. It was the door of the shopkeeper's home, and the shopkeeper's wife came to answer it.

'A very good morning to you, my dear,' said the old lady to her benignly. 'I seem to have overtaxed my strength this morning and feel rather faint. Could you kindly give me a drink of water, and allow me to come in and rest for a while?'

'But of course, Auntie!' was the prompt response.

'Come right in and make yourself comfortable.'

The shopkeeper's wife then led the old lady to her sitting-room, and when she had helped her on to a settee, she went to get her a drink of water.

But no sooner had she left the room than the old lady took the parcel of silk from underneath her shawl, and laid it on the settee beside her, partially concealed by the centre cushions which served as an arm-rest. Then, after drinking her glass of water and exchanging a few civilities with her hostess, she got up and took her leave.

At the end of the day, when the shopkeeper returned home from work, he went round to the sitting-room, as was his habit, for a few minutes relaxation before supper. And as he swept aside the centre cushions of the settee to give himself more stretching room, he discovered the wrapped up parcel of silk and wondered if his wife had gone out shopping that day?

But when he mentioned it to her over supper, she said: 'No, I was much too busy to leave the house today.'

'Then did you have any visitors?'

'No,' she said again, adding hastily, 'that is to say, not visitors in the usual way; just an old lady who came knocking at the door asking for a drink of water and wanting to rest for a while.'

'Well, it looks as if she's left her parcel behind. We'd better make sure it's nothing perishable.'

Accordingly, when supper was over and his wife was busy in the kitchen clearing up, the shopkeeper returned to the sitting-room to find out what was in the parcel.

He tore off the wrapper, and as the contents came into view, a vague feeling of apprehension stirred within him. With a quickening pulse he shook out the length of silk, and when he saw the burnt cigarette holes all along the selvedge of the material, it was as if all the bugles of hell had suddenly blared out to him the cruel truth of his wife's unfaithfulness.

Great Allah in Heaven! So it was *she,* his own wife, with whom that old lady's son was hopelessly in love! *She,* his own wife, on whom he was frittering away his youth and his money! She, she, she. . . !

Incensed with jealousy and blind fury, he rushed into the kitchen, and without a word of explanation, seized his wife and rained cruel blows upon her, calling her a liar, a cheat and a whore.

In vain did the poor woman try to defend herself, weeping, protesting and swearing by all that was holy in Heaven above and on the earth beneath, that she was innocent of all the accusations her husband was heaping upon her. But the more she wept and pleaded, the more the husband beat and abused her.

Finally he expended his fury breaking, kicking and smashing every object within his reach, to the great concern of the neighbours and passers-by who crowded outside the house convinced that the shopkeeper had suddenly gone stark raving mad.

'Well!' said the old crone who stood next to Iblees, contemplating from across the road the havoc and devastation she had created. 'What do you think of my achievement?'

'Brilliant!' chuckled Iblees. 'Absolutely brilliant! All the she-devils in hell, put together, couldn't have achieved any better!'

'Huh!' conceded the old crone. And what would you say if I told you that I could bring those two together, cooing and loving again, in no more time than it took me to destroy their happiness?'

'Ho-ho-ho!' mocked Iblees. 'Not you, nor all the Archangels in Heaven, put together, could ever achieve such a miracle!'

'Watch me then!' flung the old crone back at him, 'and be ready to eat the words you've just uttered before noontime tomorrow.'

With that, she once again turned her back squarely

upon him, and went stumping off to her home.

Next morning she set about transforming herself into the respectable old lady of the day before, and walked serenely into the busy silkshop across the road.

This time the shopkeeper didn't perceive her. He was too engrossed in his own thoughts. But the old lady had a full view of his face, and it was as dark as a thundercloud on the point of bursting. Nonetheless, she went up to him and said suavely:

'A good morning to you, son. I don't seem to have had much luck with that length of silk I bought from you yesterday. First, I stupidly burn holes in it with my cigarette, and next, I go and forget it on the sofa in your living-room. My son was furious with me, I can tell you, for he had intended taking it to his lady-love last night. But what could I do? I nearly collapsed from the heat walking up the road when I left you. . . . Luckily, I knocked at the right door for a little rest and a cold drink of water. . . . Your wife was most kind. . . .'

The shopkeeper who had been listening darkly to her in the beginning, now felt as if all the angels in Heaven had suddenly thrown the gates of paradise wide open before him.

'Pray do not mention it, Madam,' he said all smiles and bows again. 'And now you have come to retrieve your parcel?'

'Indeed I have son. But, oh this heat! It takes it out of me! Can I please ask you to send one of your boys to get the parcel for me whilst I sit here for a few minutes and take the weight off my feet?'

'But of course, Madam! How thoughtless of me not to have suggested it.' Solicitously he led her to the plush-covered settee, and with a heart overflowing with joy, continued: 'Now, you just sit here quietly, and I myself will go and get your parcel for you. I know exactly where to find it.'

He then ran all the way to his home, and when he had

located the parcel and handed it over to the old lady, he ran all the way back again and swept his wife in his arms, kissing and caressing her, and reviling himself for being a brute and a monster, and begging her on bended knees to forgive him and take him back to her heart.

And the wife who loved her husband dearly, readily forgave him and took him back to her heart, warmly returning his kisses and caresses, to the utter disgust of Iblees who saw in that picture of happy reconciliation, the definite end to all his devilish machinations.

And, not wishing to be made to eat his words by the old crone whom he saw come stumping fast towards him, he swiftly drew in his horns, and spirited himself to the nethermost regions of the earth.

Wise sayings for a thousand dinars each

There was once a prosperous merchant and he had an only son whom he was anxious to make his business partner. But first he must gauge the business acumen of the lad. So he bought him 1000 dinars' worth of goods one day, and said to him: 'If you can sell these goods at a handsome profit, I shall make you my business partner.'

The son eagerly accepted the challenge for there was nothing he coveted more than to become a partner in his father's going concern. So he packed his goods bright and early the following day, and journeyed forth to sell them in all the neighbouring towns and villages. Luck favoured him, and in less time than he had anticipated he was able to sell them at a 100 per cent profit.

Delighted with his success he made ready to return

home and receive his father's warm appraisal. But with 2000 dinars safely tucked away in his waistband, he felt he could take time off for a day's pleasure.

Accordingly, he indulged in a lazy morning in bed, and after a protracted breakfast in one of the town's principal cafés, he took a leisurely stroll through the streets and alley-ways, and stopped to look at all the shops and souks and bazaars.

By early afternoon he came to the market-place where a great crowd attracted his attention. And, curious to know what was happening, the young man pushed his way to the centre of the crowd, and there he saw a wizened old man squatting on a strip of matting, and offering to sell wise sayings at 1000 dinars each.

'A thousand dinars for a wise saying?' cried the young man incredulously. 'And what can a man achieve in life with a mere wise saying?'

'You never can tell,' said the wizened old man. 'Life is full of surprises, and a wise word spoken at the right time could well be a life-saver.'

These words greatly impressed the young man. He sat aside, and after mulling them over for a while, he decided to buy one wise saying. So he counted 1000 dinars out of his waistband and asked the old man to sell him a wise saying.

The old man looked at him long and keenly, and then said, 'Repeat after me: "Take to your heart the beloved who loves you, though he be a monkey".'

The young man repeated the words after him, then he repeated them over and over to himself, but failed to find how they could possibly benefit him in any way in life.

'Is that all you could sell me?' he expostulated. 'Whatever am I to do with words of love and the beloved? You could have at least sold me something which would help reduce any obstacles or difficulties I am likely to come up against in life.'

'If love and the beloved are in your heart, any obstacles or difficulties you are likely to come up against in life would be considerably reduced, if not altogether removed,' was the dispassionate reply.

But these words of wisdom failed to satisfy the young man who now bitterly regretted his rashness in paying out such a large sum of money for something as abstract as a wise saying. What could he now do to recover his loss?

'In business,' his father had once said to him, 'if you lose on one deal, do not panic. Try, rather, to recover your loss by attempting another deal.'

Having thus reflected, the young man now felt entirely justified in risking another 1000 dinars in the hope that he might thus be able to recover the one thousand he had just lost. So he counted out of his waistband his second 1000 dinars and asked the old man to sell him another wise saying.

Again the old man looked at him long and keenly. Then he said, 'Repeat after me: "Do not betray him who trusts you, though you be a betrayer".'

The young man repeated the words after him, then he repeated them slowly over to himself, but once again he failed to see what benefit he could derive from them. However, having now lost all his money, there was nothing more he could do about it.

So, sad and dejected he left the market-place, and since he couldn't possibly now think of returning home and facing his father empty-handed, he decided to stay where he was and look for work.

The day was then fast drawing to a close, and anxious to find himself shelter before darkness set in, the young man walked through the streets of the town and knocked at every door he came to, offering his services in return for a night's shelter. But he had no success.

Finally he came to a mill. And the miller, an ailing old man who was in fact looking for a young lad to help him with the heavy work at the mill, was only too glad to give him shelter for the night in return for his services the next day.

But, thought the miller to himself, would the lad be still alive the next day? So far, every young man he had taken on and left to spend a night at the mill, had been found dead the next morning. And the cause of death continued to be a mystery. Would this young man then fare any better than his predecessors? The miller had grave doubts.

Nonetheless he took him in, and without telling him anything about the fate of those who had preceded him, he gave him a loaf of bread and shook out a couple of empty flour sacks for him to sleep on. Then he locked up the mill and left him.

The young man ate the bread and stretched himself out on the empty flour sacks, but found it hard to go to sleep. Towards midnight he heard some stealthy movement in the mill, and got up to investigate. He then came face to face with a great black *jinn* who held a young woman in each of his hands. One woman was fair and beautiful, the other was dark and ugly.

'Now young man,' said the *jinn* without any preliminaries, 'these two women are my wives. Which of the two do you think I should love best?'

The young man was in a dilemma. 'If I say, "the beautiful one",' he thought to himself, 'the *jinn* will take offence at my having passed over his ugly wife. And if I say, "the ugly one," he may object to my not approving of his taste in women. What to do?'

Suddenly the first wise saying he had bought earlier in the day flashed through his mind. 'Take to your heart the beloved who loves you, though he be a monkey,' he said aloud to the *jinn*.

'Wisely spoken,' said the *jinn*, 'and with these words you have saved your life; for, had you said "the beautiful one", or "the ugly one", I would have killed

you as I have killed all those before you who had made that foolish mistake.' With that, he disappeared.

Early next morning the old miller came to open his mill, and great was his surprise and relief to find the young man still alive. But, how had he managed to escape the fate of all those who had preceded him?

Warily, he began asking him questions: Did he sleep well? Did he see or hear anything? Had anything untoward happened during the night?

But, for some curious reason, the young man refrained from telling the miller about the appearance of the *jinn,* and what took place between them. He simply assured him that he had slept well, that he did not see or hear anything, and that nothing untoward had happened during the night.

The miller was very thankful, but his curiosity remained unsatisfied. However, as he needed help badly, he readily offered to keep the young man on if he wished to continue working for him.

The young man in turn, penniless and destitute as he now was, and not wishing to go back home before he had made good his father's loss, eagerly accepted the offer.

In the days that followed, he worked hard and conscientiously, and little by little, the miller came to depend upon him more and more. Before long, he not only put him in full control of the mill, but he also lodged him in his own home, and having no progeny of his own, treated him like a son. And so the seasons followed one after the other, and all was serene.

Then, one day, the miller decided to go on a pilgrimage to the Hejaz and offered to take his wife with him. But the wife declined the offer on the plea that the journey would be too arduous for her. The miller, on reflection, thought that it would too. So he left her behind, after warmly entrusting her to the care of the young man, and set forth on his journey, content and secure in his mind that both his business and his wife were in trustworthy hands.

Now the miller's wife was young and beautiful. And it was not because the journey to the Hejaz would have proved too arduous for her that she had declined to accompany her husband, but it was because she secretly had an eye on the young man, and was determined to have him during her husband's absence.

No sooner was the coast clear therefore, than she started deploying all her wiles and charms to seduce the young man. But the young man had no designs on his employer's wife, and politely but firmly, rebuffed all her advances.

This only served to incense the lady even more. So she doubled and redoubled her manœuvres, but all to no avail.

Finally, one night, when she had decked herself out in a most tantalizing manner, she surprised the young man in his bedroom and begged him to take her.

The temptation was great, for no man is an angel. And Iblees who hovers in the background ever ready to bring about the final downfall in such circumstances, whispered hotly in his ear: 'Take her . . . don't be a fool . . . her husband is far away . . . he'll never know . . . he trusts you. . . .'

In a flash, the second wise saying he had bought months earlier, shot through the young man's mind: 'Do not betray him who trusts you, though you be a betrayer.'

Without a moment's hesitation he sprang out of bed and carried the lady bodily out of his bedroom. And, from then on, to safeguard against any such future incursions, he kept his bedroom door locked day and night.

For this great humiliation the lady never forgave him, and secretly swore to have her revenge. So, as soon as her husband returned from the Hejaz, she accused the young man of having attempted to seduce her, and insisted that he be dismissed altogether from the mill.

The miller was greatly grieved to hear this, for he had placed implicit faith and trust in the young man. At the same time, he had to admit that the young man had proved, all along, to be absolutely worthy of his trust. But, in the face of his wife's emphatic accusations, he had no other choice than to dismiss him. And he told him so.

Now the young man who had grown to be very fond of the old miller, and held him in the same regard as he would a parent, couldn't possibly think of leaving him under the impression that he had betrayed his trust. He, therefore, told him the whole story, starting from the time he had left his father's home to sell his 1000 dinars' worth of goods, to the time he had bought the two wise sayings in the market-place, and on to the appearance of the *jinn* and what took place between the n that first night he had spent in the mill.

And the miller, who had never ceased to puzzle over the enigma as to how this young man could have escaped the fate of all those who had preceded him, readily believed him. For he now finally understood how they came to die.

So he took back the young man to whom he now signed over the full possession of the mill, and sent his wife packing back to her father's home – a sadly divorced and humiliated woman.

The rashness of the young and the wisdom of the old

There was once an old man and he had a daughter who was the apple of his eye. But he had so pampered and indulged her, that she grew up wilful and spoilt, and determined to have her way in everything.

When she became of marriageable age, the father, who was anxious to see her well settled during his lifetime, set about choosing for her one suitor after the other from amongst the best families in the land. But the daughter turned them all down, declaring that she would only marry the man of her choice – a handsome upstanding young fellow, with no fortune to his name, but plenty of will-power and determination.

The father had his qualms about the suitability of such a union, for the young man, resolute and determined as he was, would be hardly likely to put up with his daughter's many tantrums. But as she had set her heart upon him, the father knew that nothing he would say or do would make her change her mind.

So, the wedding was celebrated with great pomp and rejoicing, and after forty days and nights of gay festivities, the bride was escorted to her husband's home in grand style.

A couple of moons thus passed, and all was milk and honey. Then came the day when the daughter had her first flare-up with her husband. And, pampered and indulged as she was, she left him in a huff and fled to her father's home in a welter of tears, loudly lamenting the selfishness and cruelty of her husband, and promising never again to return to him.

The father who knew his daughter well, and had in fact secretly anticipated such an occurrence, didn't take her lament too seriously. He, however, did his best to soothe and comfort her, so that by the end of the day when her husband called to make it up and take her back home, she had worn her huff out and didn't require too much pressure to accompany him.

So, all was milk and honey once again. But before many more moons had passed, the daughter had a second flare-up with her husband, and this was followed by a series of successive others, each of which provided a legitimate excuse for her to leave her home and go fleeing to her father, weeping and wailing about the inconsiderate way in which her husband treated her and threatening, each time, never to return to him again.

The husband took it all very patiently at first, but finally his patience ran out. And one day when his wife had left him after yet another flare-up, he went round to the father and expressed to him his great distaste for these recurrent matrimonial squabbles, and his hot indignation at the way his wife persisted in crossing his wishes and refusing to recognize and submit to his authority as a husband. 'For unless she is willing to do so,' he concluded decisively, 'she need never bother to come back to me again.'

The father was greatly disturbed to hear this, though he was fully on his son-in-law's side: a wife *must* submit to her husband's wishes, and recognize his authority. But how was he going to put this across to his daughter? At the first mention of such a condition as obedience and submission to her husband's authority, she would flauntingly rebel and thus, in her rashness, wreck her marriage. 'And that,' thought the father decisively to himself, 'is what I must prevent at all costs.'

Aloud he said to the husband: 'I am fully on your side. But before we go any further, let me ask you a question. Do you still love your wife?'

'No man could love woman more,' said the husband.

'That's all I wanted to know,' said the father. 'Now listen to me, and if you do as I tell you, I promise you that your wife will never again leave your side, nor will she ever again question your authority. For the time being, just go home and leave the rest to me. I will tell you when it's time to come and take her back.'

With that, he ushered the husband out and went to join his daughter. 'Daughter,' he said, 'your husband came to make it up and take you back home. But I refused to let you go; not for a few more days anyway. That should be a lesson to your husband to treat you with more consideration in future.'

'O father,' said the daughter, glad to see that he was fully on her side, 'you always think of the right thing to say.'

After that, they spent the rest of the evening chatting chummily together, and before they separated for the night the father said:

'You know, daughter, since you were married no one has thought of giving me an early morning gourd of fresh milk, straight from the cow's udders.'

'O father,' said the daughter, 'tomorrow you shall have an early morning gourd of fresh milk, straight from the cow's udders.'

And at break of dawn the next day, the daughter went to the cowshed to milk the cow, and took to her father an early morning gourd of fresh milk, straight from the cow's udders.

The father made great play of his early morning gourd of fresh milk, and at the end of the day he said to his daughter:

'You know, daughter, since you were married no one has thought of giving me pancakes for breakfast.'

'O father,' said the daughter, 'tomorrow you shall have pancakes for breakfast.'

And at break of dawn the next day, when she had milked the cow for her father's early morning gourd of fresh milk, the daughter got busy on the pancakes for his breakfast.

The father ate his pancakes and blessed his daughter, and at the end of the day he said to her:

'You know, daughter, since you were married no one has thought of giving me a stuffed shoulder of lamb for dinner.'

'O father,' said the daughter, 'tomorrow you shall have a stuffed shoulder of lamb for dinner.'

And at break of dawn the next day, when she had milked the cow for her father's early morning gourd of fresh milk, and had prepared pancakes for his breakfast, she got busy on the stuffed shoulder of lamb for his dinner.'

The father made short work of his stuffed shoulder of lamb, and when he had licked his fingers clean, he said to his daughter:

'You know, daughter, since you were married no one has thought of giving me a pair of tender roast pigeons for supper.'

'O father,' said the daughter, 'tomorrow you shall have a pair of tender roast pigeons for supper.'

And at break of dawn the next day, when she had milked the cow for her father's early morning gourd of fresh milk, and had prepared pancakes for his breakfast, and a stuffed shoulder of lamb for his dinner, she got busy on the roast pigeons for his supper.'

The father did full honours to his pair of tender roast pigeons, and, at the end of the day, content and replete, said to his daughter:

'You know, daughter, since you got married no one has thought of giving my outdoor *jubba* (coat) a good wash for me.'

'O father,' said the daughter, 'tomorrow I shall give your outdoor *jubba* a good wash for you.'

And at break of dawn the next day, when she had milked the cow for her father's early morning gourd of fresh milk, and had prepared pancakes for his breakfast, a stuffed shoulder of lamb for his dinner, and a pair of tender roast pigeons for his supper, she got busy washing his outdoor *jubba* for him.

And so it went on. Every day the father would add yet another chore to his daughter's crowded schedule, so that by the end of fourteen days she was so utterly exhausted that she could hardly sit up with him in the evenings.

'Good!' thought the father. 'Now is the time to send for the husband.' And he did so. The husband came, and this is what the father said to him:

'You and I will be having supper on our own. And after supper, I want you to slip quietly round to my bedroom, without seeing my daughter, and spend the night there.'

The husband opened his mouth to ask one of a dozen questions which were burning on his lips, but the father gave him no chance. 'Do not question me please. Just do exactly as I tell you.'

So, after supper the two men separated, and the father then went round to the kitchen where his daughter was still busy clearing up.

'Daughter,' he said, 'I feel rather tired tonight, and will retire early. So I'll leave you to your husband. He'll be waiting for you in your bedroom.'

The daughter dutifully expressed her concern about her father's state of health, and after wishing him a very good night, she hastily finished her kitchen chores and went round to her bedroom, eagerly anticipating a fond reunion with her husband after so many days of separation.

To her great mortification, however, instead of finding him awake and alert and burning with impatience to receive her, she found him in bed, fast asleep, as was evident from the deep snores that resounded from beneath the white cotton sheet he had pulled right over his head. At that, her anger and frustration got the better of her.

'You shameless, heartless man,' she said, with none too gentle a poke at the recumbent figure in the bed. 'You could have at least had the decency to sit up and wait to welcome me. But of course, you couldn't. . . . How could you. . . ! You had to hide your face in shame, leaving me behind all of fourteen days to toil and slave from dawn to dusk for my old fool of a father, until I hardly know if I am standing on my head or my heels. . . .'

But all the response she got was a succession of deeper snores. This infuriated her even more, and as she proceeded to undress for the night, she gave vent to the anger which mounted higher and higher within her, by mimicking her old father's quavering voice: 'Daughter, since you got married no one has thought of giving me an early morning gourd of fresh milk, straight from the cow's udders. . . . Daughter, since you got married, no one has thought of giving me pancakes for break-fast. . . . Daughter, since you got married no one has thought of giving me a stuffed shoulder of lamb for dinner. . . . Daughter this. . . . Daughter that. . . ! The crazy old fool. . . ! What does he take me for, a beast of burden? And you, you cruel, stone-hearted man. . . . It never once occurred to you to come and rescue me. . . . But wait! I haven't finished with you yet. . . . I'll settle you in the morning. . . .'

Having thus exploded her anger, and utterly disdain-ing all closer contact with her husband's recumbent figure, she curled up at the foot of the bed, and went to sleep.

Early next morning as the events of the night before began forcing themselves slowly on her waking consciousness, she sat up with a jerk in bed, ready to flay her erring husband with the sharp edge of her tongue.

But it was not the face of her erring husband on which her blazing eyes fell. It was the serene face of her old father, still in peaceful slumber, his long grey beard gently rising and falling to his rhythmic breathing, over the white cotton sheet which was now firmly tucked beneath his chin.

In a flash, the enormity of what she had done hit her like a thunderclap. With one bound she was out of bed and sprinting across the hall to her father's bedroom where her husband was still asleep.

'Wake up! Wake up!' she cried, shaking him hysterically by the shoulders. 'I've done a most awful thing! I can't stay here a moment longer! You must take me back home . . . now, this very minute. . . .'

The husband who was quick to surmise what had happened, saw his opportunity and seized it. 'I will only take you back if you give me your solemn promise, here and now, that you will never again cross my will, and never again question my authority.'

'I promise! I promise!' she cried, dragging him bodily out of bed. 'You can beat me up, you can wipe the floor with me, you can do anything you like, but take me back home . . . take me back home. . . .'

And, chuckling inwardly to himself, but with a great outward show of purpose and determination, the husband bundled his wife back home, and she never again left his side, and never again questioned his authority.

The farmer who found his match in his daughter-in-law

There was once a farmer who was obdurate and astute in his business dealings, and he had a son to whom he was always setting a tricky problem.

The son, a dreamy romantic lad, had none of the business astuteness of his father, and he didn't relish the tricky problems with which he constantly plagued him. But he always did his best to placate him.

One day, the son asked his father for permission to get married. But the father said he would give his permission only if the son could prove to him that he was capable of driving a good business bargain all on his own.

'And how am I to prove this to you?' queried the son.

'I will tell you,' said the father. 'Take this sheep; and if you can sell it live for the highest price obtainable on the market and, at the same time, retain one pound of its meat and one pound of its bones, you will have proved to me without a doubt that you are as astute a business man as anyone could wish to be.'

'But how can you expect me to sell a sheep, live, for the highest price obtainable on the market and, at the same time, retain one pound of its meat and one pound of its bones?' argued the son.

'Aha!' was the father's tantalizing retort. 'Therein lies your test.'

The son argued no more. He led out of the pen the sheep his father had singled out to him, and drove it to the next village where the seasonal market for goats and sheep was being held.

The farmer who found his match in his daughter-in-law

On the way to the village, he joined up with a prosperous looking merchant, and when the two had exchanged greetings and the habitual niceties which follow, the boy said to the merchant: 'Shall we associate together?'

The merchant, noticing that the boy had nothing but a single sheep, politely declined.

The boy didn't seem to mind the rebuff, and walked cheerfully on, alongside the merchant. After a while, they met a funeral procession.

'Do you think the man in the coffin is dead, or does he still live?' asked the boy.

'He is dead, of course!' said the merchant thinking to himself: 'What an odd question!'

Soon after they passed the funeral procession, they came across a man who was strewing seeds along a line of newly ploughed furrows.

'Do you think the man is planting, or is he a planter?' again the boy asked.

'If he is planting he is a planter,' said the merchant beginning to wonder if the boy was all there.

A little further on they came to a stream which they had to cross. The merchant promptly took off his *markoob,* and held them up high and dry as he waded barefoot into the water. But the boy kept his *markoob* on as he waded across.

What an odd thing to do, again thought the merchant to himself, and was secretly relieved when they finally reached the village, so as to be rid of the boy. Being the older man, however, he could not very well disregard the customary rules of hospitality which prompted him to offer shelter to the boy for the night. The boy thanked him but declined the offer, saying that he was spending the night 'in the home of the people'.

With that, he bade the merchant good-night, and departed leading his sheep behind him.

That night, when he was back home, the merchant

recounted to his daughter his encounter with the boy, and his odd behaviour.

But the daughter didn't seem to think that the boy's behaviour was odd in any way. 'On the contrary,' she said, 'he sounds like a bright intelligent lad to me.'

But the father would have none of it. 'How can you say he is bright and intelligent,' he expostulated, 'when hardly knowing me, and possessing nothing but a single sheep, he has the nerve to ask me to associate with him?'

'He only meant it in a social, not a financial sense,' countered his daughter. 'Don't you see? You were two solitary travellers walking along a road in the same direction, and all the boy meant to say, was, "let us walk together and be sociable".'

The father considered this possibility in silence. Then he said: 'You may be right. But how would you explain his question as to whether the man who was being carried in a coffin to his grave, was dead or still lived?'

'Because,' said his daughter, 'if that man has children, he is not dead; he still lives – in his children.'

'Huh!' grunted the father, when he had mulled this over for a while. 'You have a point there. But how about the man who was strewing seeds along a line of newly ploughed furrows. Couldn't the boy see he was planting?'

'Of course he could. But he couldn't know if he was a hired hand – planting, or, if he was the owner of the land – a planter.'

'H'm!' conceded the father grudgingly. 'You certainly seem to have found the answer to all the riddles. But just explain to me this last one: why did the boy keep his *markoob* on when we crossed the stream, instead of taking them off as I did, to prevent them from getting soaked?'

'I will tell you,' said the daughter. 'Because the bed of the stream is very often full of sharp stones and rusty nails; or jagged pieces of glass and the like, any of which

64

could have cut his feet had he waded across without the protection of his *markoob*. You were lucky to come out unscathed. So you see, my father,' she concluded on a triumphant note, 'that boy is not half as odd as you think he is, and it is a pity you didn't bring him home with you. Where did you say he was spending the night?'

'In the home of the people, whatever that may mean,' said the father.

'That means the mosque,' said the daughter. 'And he must be hungry, for he is not likely to find any food in the mosque at this time of night. So come, my father, take this small basket of food to him, and invite him to come and sup with us tomorrow night.'

With that, she packed a few hardboiled eggs and some pancakes into a basket, and handed them over to her father, together with a freshly filled water *gulla*.

On his way to the mosque the father met a beggar. 'Hasana lillah!' (Alms for the love of God), pleaded the beggar, grovelling in the dust at the merchant's feet.

Moved by the beggar's plea, the merchant stopped and gave him two eggs and four pancakes. He then handed him the water *gulla* from which he took a long draught to slake his thirst. After that, the merchant proceeded to the mosque where the boy had not yet settled for the night.

'Greetings,' said the merchant to him. 'I bring you a little food and fresh water, and an invitation from my daughter to come and sup with us tomorrow night.'

The boy expressed his gratitude to the merchant, and after helping himself to a few eggs and some pancakes, he took a refreshing draught from the *gulla,* and then said:

'Please thank your daughter for her hospitality, and tell her that the year lacked two months, and the month lacked four days, and the river was at low ebb.'

Mystified, the merchant repeated all this to his

daughter when he returned home, and asked her if she understood what it all meant.

'Perfectly!' she laughed. 'But first tell me. Who was it you met on your way to the mosque?'

'A beggar,' affirmed the father.

'And you gave him two eggs and four pancakes?'

'In the name of Allah! How could you tell?' exclaimed the father.

'From the message you just brought me,' again laughed the daughter, and as the father continued to listen to her, more and more mystified, she went on to say: 'I told you, didn't I, that the lad sounded quite bright and intelligent to me? What I didn't tell you is that I felt sure he must be quite romantic too! But first I had to prove that to myself. So I thought I would try him out with the language of symbols. I therefore sent him twelve eggs to symbolize a year of twelve months, and since his message to me was "the year lacked two months", it meant that two eggs were missing. Then I sent him thirty pancakes to symbolize a month of thirty days, and since he told you "the month lacked four days", it meant that four pancakes were missing. Finally, I filled the water *gulla* up to the brim to symbolize a fully flowing river, and since he said "the river was at low ebb", it meant that someone else had drunk from the *gulla* before him.'

'Upon my word,' thought the father, 'I do believe my daughter has fallen for the lad before she set eyes on him!'

But the idea did not at all perturb him, for he was anxious to see her happily married and well settled during his lifetime.

So, bright and early next morning, he set out for the mosque to look for the boy and take him home to meet his daughter. But the boy had already gone to market and was having a difficult time trying to sell his sheep on the lines laid down by his father. For not one of the many buyers who would have readily paid the best possible price for it, would hear of letting him retain a pound of its meat and a pound of its bones before parting with it.

'How like my father to set me such a thorny problem,' thought the boy, as he returned to the mosque with his unsold sheep, feeling dejected and dismayed.

There he found the merchant waiting for him, and not wishing to leave his sheep unattended behind, he took it with him to the merchant's home.

The merchant's daughter received him with a warm welcome, and as soon as he saw her the boy fell deeply in love with her for she was very beautiful and he wanted to marry her. But he knew he couldn't do this until he had solved the thorny problem his father had set him, and the thought made him silent and despondent.

The merchant's daughter noticed his despondency and asked him what the trouble was. The boy told her his story. She listened to him attentively, then said: 'Your father must be a very astute business man. However, the problem he has set you is not insolvable.'

The boy looked at her hopefully. 'How would *you* solve it?' he asked eagerly.

'Well,' she said deliberately, 'first I would shear the sheep. Then I would spin the wool and fashion it into a nice warm scarf. And, as pure woollen scarves are in great demand, this, on its own, should fetch almost half the price of the live sheep on the market. Then, I would saw off the sheep's horns, and these (as she surveyed them critically) should weigh one pound. So there you have your one pound of bones. Then, I would cut off the sheep's tail, and that, (as she manipulated it knowingly) should also weigh one pound. So there you have your one pound of meat too. Now, I would take the sheep to market, and, tail-less and horn-less though it be, it should still fetch a good price, for it is young and fat and home bred.

'Thus you will find that the price of the blemished sheep, added to the price of the scarf fashioned out of its wool, would exceed by a handsome margin, even your father's most ambitious expectations.'

'By Allah!' cried the boy in jubilation. 'I do believe my father has finally met his match in you!'

Next day, he did exactly as the merchant's daughter had suggested, and hurried back home with the best price any farmer, no matter how astute, could have ever hoped to obtain for a tail-less, horn-less sheep.

The farmer was delighted with his son's success which he vaingloriously attributed to his own method of sharpening the lad's wits by continually setting him a tricky problem to solve, and readily gave him permission to get married.

So the boy married the merchant's daughter and brought her to his father's home. The father made her right welcome. But before many days had passed, he had little doubt that it was she who had solved the problem of the sheep for his son.

That was a severe blow to his vanity for he didn't like to be outwitted by a woman. For some time, therefore, he carefully refrained from setting his son a tricky problem, lest he receive another blow to his vanity.

But habit is a second nature, and one morning as he stepped jauntily out of the house on his way to the fields, he said to his son loud enough for his daughter-in-law to hear: 'I shall be working late today; so send me my midday meal to the fields with your unborn son.'

With that, he pulled the door sharply to behind him, thinking smugly to himself: 'Now, let us see how she is going to solve this one.'

The boy looked at his wife in consternation. But she didn't appear in the least perturbed. 'Let me handle this one,' she said to him, 'and don't you worry.'

Then, early that afternoon she disguised herself as the Mayor of the district, and rode out to the fields with a great show of authority. The farmer who was sowing a field of wheat saw 'the Mayor', and hastened forward to make him welcome.

The Mayor reigned in his horse, and without dismounting asked the farmer what was it he was sowing.

'A field of wheat for next season's crop, Your Excellency,' said the farmer.

'Good!' said the Mayor. 'Let me now have two sacks of this new crop of wheat.'

The farmer gave him a wide, indulgent smile. 'I beg pardon, Your Excellency, I don't seem to have made myself clear, I am only just sowing next season's crop of wheat. . . .'

'I heard you,' cut in the Mayor tersely. 'You are only just sowing next year's crop of wheat. Fine! Now I am ordering you to let me have two sacks of this new crop of wheat here and now, and no more shilly-shallying, please.'

The wide indulgent smile slowly disappeared from the farmer's face, and he looked at the Mayor with puckered brows. 'But this is virtually impossible, Your Excellency. The seed has barely sunk into the earth. . . .'

'In other words, you refuse to obey my command,' again the Mayor cut him short. 'Very well, let us see if *this* will teach you a lesson.'

Then, turning to the farmhands who, attracted by the Mayor's presence, had dropped everything and stood looking curiously on, he said sharply:

'Stretch this man out and give him ten strokes of the birch on the bare soles of his feet for disobeying my orders.'

The farmhands stretched the farmer out and gave him ten strokes of the birch on the bare soles of his feet, for who were they to disobey the Mayor's command?

69

eric fraser

The Mayor watched the birching, then rode off leaving the farmer to nurse his sore feet. In the evening he went limping back home, and his son who knew nothing of what had happened, asked him why he was limping.

'Because of the arrant stupidity of the Mayor of our district,' replied the farmer, boiling with anger. 'Fancy insisting that I produce, there and then, two sacks of next year's crop of wheat which I was only just planting! Allah! Doesn't the man realize that any seed which is planted has to take its own time to germinate and mature before it can be reaped? Just how ridiculous can a Mayor be, I ask you!'

'No less ridiculous than you are,' retorted his daughter-in-law. 'Insisting that your meal be sent to you to the fields with a grandchild who has just been conceived.'

These words had a great sobering effect on the farmer, and from that day on, he never again attempted to plague his son with a tricky problem.

The eye will see what it is destined to see . . .

There was once a rich man and he had two daughters. One was shallow and fickle and had little love for her father, but she knew how to cajole and flatter him and so make him buy her expensive presents and fill her purse with spending money.

The other was warm and kind-hearted, though pensive and reticent, and loved her father dearly. But she hardly ever asked him for anything.

'Yet there must be something which your eye desires to see,' would insist the father. To which the daughter would invariably reply: 'The eye will see what it is destined to see, my father.'

After a time, this repeated rhetoric of his daughter's irritated the father. And one day, in a fit of anger, he said to her: 'Very well! Let me now show you what your eye is destined to see.'

Precisely at that moment, a beggar came knocking at the door begging for alms. 'Here!' said the father to him. 'Take my daughter. I do not want her.'

'What will I do with your daughter?' protested the beggar. 'As it is, I can hardly subsist on the alms I receive.'

'Allah kareem!' (God will provide), said the father curtly, as he pushed his daughter out of the house, and closed the door decisively behind her.

The beggar stood irresolute for a while, waiting to see what the girl would say or do. But the girl said nothing, and when he started to move on, she followed him without a murmur or protest.

When they had walked a little way, the beggar, moved by the girl's plight, suggested that she ride the old half-starved donkey he was leading, and so save her feet from the rough dusty roads. But the girl assured him that she didn't mind the rough dusty roads, and was quite happy to walk alongside of him.

So they walked and walked, begging their way from door to door, and much to the beggar's astonishment, at every door they knocked they were met with kindness and given generous quantities of food and clean fresh water to drink, as well as a *malleem* (a small coin) or two into the bargain. Whereas, before the girl had joined him, he was frequently turned empty-handed from many a door at which he knocked, and by the end of the day the contents of his alms sack barely sufficed to fill the emptiness within him.

Small wonder then that he attributed this sudden change of luck to the presence of the girl beside him, and as the day wore on, he felt more and more kindly disposed towards her.

At noontime they stopped to rest under the shade of a tree by the roadside, and anxious to put the girl at ease, the beggar spread the contents of his alms sack at her feet, and invited her to eat her fill whilst he rested. But the girl refused to touch the food unless he joined her, and insisted moreover that they share every morsel equally together.

The beggar was deeply touched by this gesture of true comradeship, and a protective feeling for the girl which fate had so suddenly and so strangely thrust upon him, now began to possess him.

When they had eaten and rested, they took to the road again, and by late afternoon they reached the foot of a hill which overlooked a prosperous looking town. The hill was not too steep, and as the girl was now very tired and could hardly keep on her feet, the beggar took her on his donkey to the hilltop where she could rest for as long as she wished without being exposed to the eyes of the passers-by.

There he made her as comfortable as possible, and when he had tied his donkey to a stake nearby, he slung his alms sack on his back and went down the hill to investigate the 'begging' possibilities of the new town, promising to return before nightfall.

The girl was only too thankful for a little rest and privacy. Her feet were sore from trudging the hot dusty roads, and her head ached from too much exposure to the sun. But the cool evening breeze which played softly over the hilltop soon lulled her into a long refreshing sleep.

Towards sunset she woke to the loud braying of the donkey who had broken loose of his stake and was straying widely over the hilltop, cropping contentedly at the tufts of dry grass which grew sparsely here and there.

The eye will see what it is destined to see . . .

The girl ran up to him and led him back. She then picked up a stone and tried to fix his stake more firmly in the ground. But she seemed to have chosen a soft spot, for at the first hard hit of the stone, the stake disappeared into a hole, and though the girl pushed her hand deep in to recover it, she couldn't find it. Intrigued, she kept digging deeper and deeper into the hole in an attempt to recover the stake, but all to no avail.

In the end, her fingers met a hard object at which she pulled and pulled, and when she finally succeeded in dislodging it, she saw that it was a large earthenware jar and its neck was hermetically sealed with mud.

Eagerly, she knocked off the neck of the jar and tipped it over the sackcloth on which she had been resting. A cascade of gold coins and precious stones came tumbling down, winking and glinting at her like sparks of fire in the red rays of the setting sun.

The girl gazed at this treasure trove in awe and wonder. Then, lightly, almost reverently, she ran her hands over the shimmering pile, probing it with her fingers here and there as if to make sure of its solidity and genuineness.

For a long time she sat thus, silent and pensive, contemplating her newly found riches. Then she drew a corner of her sackcloth lightly over them, and waited for the beggar to return.

He returned as he had promised, shortly before nightfall. And his alms sack was bulging with the bits and pieces he had succeeded in begging for their supper: there was bread and cheese and an onion; a head of *faseekh* (salted fish), a few pickled turnips, and a handful of dates and peanuts.

Cheerfully, almost jovially, the beggar spread this meagre feast before the girl, and as they sat side by side sharing it together, he recounted to her his impression of the new town and its inhabitants: 'On the whole, they seem to be a pretty decent lot,' he said contentedly. 'For at every door I knocked I was given a little something, and spoken to with kindness. You'll see for yourself when we go on our first begging tour tomorrow. And if you like the place, too, I see no reason why we shouldn't remain here for as long as we can beg a living.'

The girl listened to him without interruption. And when he had finished speaking, she said to him lightly: 'Tell me, my friend, what would you do if you suddenly came into possession of 1000 rials?'

'I would feed one beggar for a whole year,' said the beggar unhesitatingly.

'And for 2000 rials you would presumably feed two beggars for the same period of time?' again queried the girl.

'That is so,' affirmed the beggar.

The girl was silent for a while, then she said: 'What if it were 5000 rials?'

'For 5000 rials,' said the beggar, 'I would go to the mosque every Friday noon and feed all the beggars that would be gathered there for midday prayers.'

A longer pause here ensued, then the girl again resumed: 'But supposing it were much more than 5000 rials; say, ten, twenty, fifty, a hundred, or even a thousand times more, what would you do?'

This time the beggar's answer was not so readily forthcoming. He pondered the question for a long while, then said: 'For that much money I would build a home where all the beggars in the land would come for free to eat and rest and wash themselves clean from the dust and sweat of the road, whenever they felt the need.'

A soft sigh of contentment from the girl indicated her full approval of this charitable idea. 'And would you vow, before Allah, that you would do all this, were you indeed to become so rich?' was her next eager query.

'Before Allah, I vow I would,' affirmed the beggar;

75

then added on a more realistic tone: 'But how am I ever likely to fulfil such a vow? Will my eye ever see such riches?'

'The eye will see what it is destined to see, my friend,' said the girl quietly, and shifting her position slightly, she drew back the corner of the sackcloth on which they were resting, and revealed to the beggar her treasure trove.

The beggar gazed dumbfounded at the glittering pile. Then he turned to the girl and said: 'These riches are all yours. You found them. I have no claim to them whatsoever. So dispose of them in any way you like; and if you wish to leave me now, and set yourself up in a home of your own. . . .'

'We shall set up a home of our own together,' interposed the girl, 'and we shall share these riches together, in the same way that we have shared the alms we have begged together.'

'But you are now richer than any Sultan's daughter,' argued the beggar, 'and the handsomest and richest princes in the land would fain ride over each other for the chance of wooing you. Why then should you want to link your destiny to mine? In the final count I am only a beggar.'

'Before Allah we are all beggars,' countered the girl. 'And for that matter, what was I but a beggar the day my father thrust me out of the house and you readily took me on? But since it is Allah alone who reduces the rich to beggary, and raises the beggars to riches, who are we to refute the riches he has now so generously bestowed upon us?'

The beggar had no ready answer to this, but the girl could feel that he remained unconvinced. It was only after a long earnest talk which took them far into the night, that she finally succeeded in demolishing, step by step, every social barrier he attempted to raise between them.

The eye will see what it is destined to see . . .

And so, hardly able to realize that they need never ever go begging again, the beggar and the girl curled up on their sackcloth and went to sleep.

Next morning they were up with the crowing cock, and when the sun had flooded the hilltop, they rode their donkey to the town below, and treated themselves to the most gorgeous feed money could buy. They then spent the rest of the morning exploring souks and bazaars, and wound up in the market-place where they bought themselves everything that took their fancy.

After that, they went to look for the Mayor of the town and informed him of their wish to buy the hill which overlooked the town. The Mayor, anticipating the customary amount of haggling and bargaining over such an important deal, named a pretty high price. But the beggar neither haggled nor bargained. He paid the price named, and walked out of the Mayor's presence the rightful owner of the hill where the fates had thus led him.

The way was now clear before him to proceed with the fulfilment of his vow. And, since 'money is the prompt executor of all plans and projects', as the saying goes, before many moons had passed, a Beggars' Home such as had no precedence in the East or West, rose proudly on the hilltop – a haven of peace and security for the hungry and naked, and the old and ailing; and its fame spread far and wide into the land.

And so, the years came and went, bringing much more happiness to the beggar and the girl who now became his wife, and many more blessings in a houseful of sons and daughters.

What of the father and his other daughter? She had made a rich marriage and lived in opulence in a palatial home. But her riches brought her no real happiness, for she was unable to bear a child. And though she went from doctor to doctor, and from charm-maker to charm-maker, in the hope that they would make her fruitful, it was all to no avail. In the meantime the husband who, like every man of substance was anxious to have a son and heir, was getting more and more impatient and threatening to find himself a more fruitful wife.

As to the father, ever since he had turned his daughter over to the beggar, his luck began to desert him: his health failed, his friends cold-shouldered him, his business declined, the money lenders refused to extend him any further credit, and ruin finally stared him in the face.

It was then that he thought of appealing to his rich daughter for help. But all the help his rich daughter could offer him was a room in the basement of her palatial home, and a meal at the table of her kitchen staff. This made him feel thoroughly humiliated, but having no other choice, he accepted the offer.

After a time, however, he felt he could take it no longer. 'My daughter treats me like a beggar,' he thought, 'but begging for begging, I'd rather take to the road.' So, at break of dawn, one morning, he slung over his shoulder the small bundle of his belongings, and walked out of his daughter's palatial home.

He had no fixed idea as to where he would go, but he was anxious to leave his hometown far behind, so as not to be embarrassed by old friends and acquaintances when he went begging from door to door. He therefore turned his back on his hometown, and walked and walked.

After two days and two nights on the road, for he was old and ailing, and had to make frequent halts by the roadside to recover his strength, he fell in with a group of beggars who were heading for the Beggars' Home, and gladly followed in their wake.

From his hilltop, our old friend the beggar saw him arrive. But he gave no sign of having recognized him. Nonetheless, he received him kindly along with the others, and when he had offered him food and made him comfortable, he went to his wife and quietly told her that her father was reduced to beggary, and had come to seek shelter in their Home.

The wife immediately got together a festive meal, and invited her father to it that evening.

Passive and resigned, the father entered her presence without recognizing her, for she sat partly veiled and surrounded by her sons and daughters.

His eyes travelled slowly round the rich apartment, and when they finally came to rest on the festive board, he broke down completely, and said: 'I never thought my eye would ever again see such an abundance of riches.'

'The eye will see what it is destined to see, my father,' said the girl, thus declaring herself to him.

At that, the father hid his face in shame and confusion. Then he was all for getting up and taking to the road again, but the daughter wouldn't let him.

'I have long been telling my children of their grandfather,' she said, leading her young brood towards him, 'and now that he has come, they are not likely ever to let him go.'

Thus was evil repaid with good, and a child sat not in judgement over her parent.

The fisherman and the prince

There was once a fisherman, and early one morning he caught a very big fish. So big, in fact, that he took it to his hut, intending to return for it when he had finished his morning's fishing, and take it to market where he felt sure it would fetch a record price.

To his great surprise, however, when he did return

for it he found neither fish nor hut. Instead, he found a palatial mansion whose mistress, he was told, was a very beautiful lady.

The fisherman asked to see her, and when he was ushered into her presence, he asked her if she knew what had happened to his hut and the fish he had left therein.

'I was the fish,' said the lady, 'and this was my home before I was transformed by a wicked ogre and thrown into the river; but in fishing me out you have broken the spell and thus restored me to my human form.'

The fisherman expressed his delight at having been the unconscious agent of such a miraculous restoration, and whilst invoking Allah's blessings on the lady and her palatial home, he couldn't help deploring the loss of his own humble abode, for he had now nowhere else to go.

As he talked, the beautiful lady couldn't take her eyes off him, for he was young and virile and easy on the eye. Neither did she once stop to consider his lowly state. She simply fell in love with him, and asked him to marry her. And who was the fisherman to refuse?

So they got married, and were it not for an unforeseen development, I would have now ended my tale with the traditional saying, 'and they lived happily together forever after'. But. . . .

Early one spring morning, the beautiful lady went for a swim, and as she stepped out of the river, straight and slender as a carnation stalk, her shining black tresses rippling over her shoulders like a costly silken mantle, the ruling Prince of the land espied her and fell hopelessly in love with her.

He immediately ordered his courtiers to find out who she was, and when they told him that she was the wife of the local fisherman, he was sick with envy and secretly resolved to eliminate the man by every means in his princely powers.

Accordingly, the fisherman was summoned to the

eric fraser

Palace the next morning, and stood before the Prince deeply apprehensive.

The Prince looked him haughtily up and down, then said: 'It is my wish that you come and see me tomorrow laughing and crying at the same time. Else, I'll have you thrown in jail.'

The fisherman panicked. For how can one laugh and cry at the same time?

'Not to worry!' said his wife. 'Put an onion in your pocket, and before you step into the Prince's presence, bash the onion with your fist and inhale it good and proper. *That* should take care of your crying. At the same time, throw back your head and laugh long and loud and you will have fulfilled the Prince's wish.'

The fisherman did exactly as his wife told him, and as he stepped into the great hall where the Prince and his courtiers were assembled, he emitted great guffaws of laughter whilst his eyes and nose smarted and streamed like two waterworks combined.

The courtiers loudly applauded the fisherman's performance, and complimented him on the admirable manner in which he had carried out the Prince's orders. So the Prince could find no excuse for jailing the fisherman. But his determination to eliminate him was as firm as ever.

So, before many days had passed, he again sent for the fisherman, and said to him: 'It is my wish that you come and see me tomorrow dressed and naked at the same time. Else, I'll have you impaled on the Palace walls.'

The fisherman trembled with fear. For how can one be dressed and naked at the same time?

'Not to worry!' again said his wife. 'Wear your fishing net right over your naked body, and the Prince will find no cause for complaint.'

The fisherman did exactly that. And, sure enough, when he stood before the Prince and his courtiers with nothing on save his fishing net, not one of them could deny that he was, in fact, dressed and naked at the same time.

So once again the Prince was foiled in his evil designs; but he wasn't going to give up so easily. He let a few days pass, then once again he sent for the fisherman and said to him: 'It is my wish that you come and see me tomorrow with a newborn babe that can tell me a story. Else, I'll cut off your head.' And this time, he thought gloatingly to himself, I have you where I want you, my man!

The fisherman left the Palace in a state of black despair. For whoever heard of a newborn babe that can talk, much less tell a story?

But here again his beautiful wife came to the rescue. 'Go to the river,' she said to him, 'and strike the water with your fishing-rod at the same spot where you fished me out. My half-sister will then appear to you. Ask her to let you have the babe which was born to her yesterday, and take him to the Palace. He will tell the Prince a story.'

The fisherman was too depressed to argue. He did exactly as he was told. And when his wife's half-sister appeared to him, he asked her to let him have the babe which was born to her the day before. She gave it him. He then took it to the Palace and stood before the Prince, cradling it in his arms.

The Prince looked at him mockingly, and said: 'Is *that* there going to tell me a story?'

'Yes, it is!' answered the babe, suddenly wriggling out of the fisherman's arms, and walking up to the Prince. 'Now step off that throne, and let me sit on it.'

The Prince was startled out of his wits, for he had never in his life heard a newborn babe talk. Meekly he stepped off his throne, and stood, as one mesmerized, before the babe who sat fair and square upon it, and began to tell this story:

83

The fisherman and the prince

'Once upon a time, there was a very rich man and he possessed acres and acres of land which yielded him, every year, a magnificent crop of wheat and barley and rice and maize. Then, one year, this rich man decided to sow all his land with sesame seeds only. The crop he reaped was a bumper one; giving him hundreds and hundreds of sacks of sesame, each sack of which was meticulously checked and weighed and then stored away. In the final count, however, it was discovered that one sack lacked one sesame seed. But instead of letting this go, the rich man insisted on having this particular sesame seed, and set all his farmhands looking for it. They did their best, but were unable to procure it for him. Nonetheless, he kept plaguing them about it, and. . . .'

'Rubbish!' here interrupted the Prince who had now got over his fright. 'Why should such a rich man insist on having that particular sesame seed when he had hundreds and hundreds of sacks of sesame at his disposal?'

'For the same reason that a Prince who has an entire Principality of beautiful ladies at his disposal, insists on having a particular one, therefore employing every unprincely means in his power to usurp her from her lawful husband,' retorted the babe.

The rebuke struck home. And this time the Prince, who was not a bad man at heart, dismissed the fisherman with full pardon, and never again attempted to separate him from his wife.

And so, as you well see, it is only now that I can conclude this tale by saying, 'and they lived happily together for ever after'.

The ten white doves

There was once a man and he had a wife who gave him ten sons and one beautiful daughter.

Then the wife died and the man married another woman to look after his home and his children, for his business often took him far away to distant lands.

But the woman he married was, unbeknown to him, a wicked witch. And she hated the children so deeply, that she was determined to get rid of them in the quickest possible way.

So one day, when the father had to go on a distant journey, no sooner was his back turned, than the stepmother cast a spell on the sons turning them into ten white doves which instantly took to space, and she chased the daughter out of the house, confining her to the dusty smelly regions of the backyard.

Then, when in due course the father returned from his journey and asked to see his children, the stepmother told him that his sons had left home to find themselves a living on their own, but that the daughter would shortly be coming in to see him.

With that, she hurriedly left the room and went to look for the girl who sat unwashed and unkempt among the fowls and goats in the backyard.

'Come and freshen yourself up before you go in to see your father,' she said to her, as she covertly threw a magic potion into a basin of water for the girl to wash in.

The girl dipped her face into the basin of water and eagerly proceeded to clean herself up. But when she had finished she became so ugly that when she went in to see her father, he was repulsed at her sight. And not knowing it was his daughter he shouted at her angrily:

'Get out of my sight you ugly creature, and don't ever let me see you again.'

Broken-hearted at the cruel way in which her father had received her, the girl ran out of the house weeping. She ran and ran until she came to a little stream which looked so cool and inviting, that she paused by it for a little rest.

The dusk of night was then beginning to fall, and as the girl had now nowhere to go, she continued to sit by the water edge, hugging her knees and wailing and sobbing, when ten white doves lit one by one close beside her. And as they touched the ground, they turned into ten handsome young men in which she instantly recognized her ten lost brothers.

Joyously she ran forward to embrace them. And they asked her why she was weeping. She then told them of how shabbily the stepmother had treated her all along, and how finally she had made her appear so ugly in her father's eyes, that when she went in to welcome him back from his journey, he chased her out of his presence and said that he never again wanted to see her.

The brothers dried her tears and did their best to comfort her. 'In any case you look as beautiful as you always were,' they told her reassuringly. 'But now since you have no home to go to, you must come and live with us across the stream where we have found good refuge in the garden of the Prince, and we will take care of you.'

The girl was only too happy to be anywhere near her brothers even though, as they informed her, they could only resume their human form from dusk to dawn. But now, how to cross the stream? She could neither swim, nor, like her brothers, fly across. So, determined not to be left behind, she sat up all night weaving herself a net from the reeds that grew along the waterfront, and at dawn the next day, when her brothers again turned into doves, the net was ready for her to lie in. Thus the

eric fraser

brothers, holding it at each end in their beak, were able to fly their sister across, and deposit her safely near the Prince's Palace. After which, they flew off and left her.

The girl wandered aimlessly around for a while, then, being tired and sleepy from her vigil the night before, she curled up in the cool shade of the overhanging branches of an acacia tree which grew within the Palace garden, and soon fell fast asleep.

Then she dreamed that an old woman came up to her and said: 'If you want your brothers to resume their human shape and never again be turned into doves, you must fashion for them ten coats out of the leaves of the acacia tree under which you are now sleeping. And when the coats are ready, you are to fit them on to the doves as and when they light near you. But, from the moment you start working on the coats, till the moment you finish them, you are to observe the strictest silence; failing which, you'll never succeed in breaking the spell your stepmother has cast upon your brothers.'

This dream was so vivid, that when she woke up the girl could still visualize the old woman speaking to her, and her words rang clear as a silver bell in her ears.

So, anxious to restore her brothers to their human shape without any loss of time, the girl picked a lapful of acacia leaves and started then and there working on the prescribed coats, observing from that moment on, the strictest silence.

Then, one day, as she sat intent upon her work by the edge of the stream, the Prince of the Palace perceived her, and attracted by the serene beauty of her face, stopped to greet her. But the girl refrained from returning his greeting; nor would she be drawn into any conversation he attempted to start with her.

Thinking she was dumb, the Prince took no offence. But he came to see her day after day, for he was bewitched by her beauty. Finally, he decided to marry her, and gave her to understand that much. The girl seemed to have no objection. So the Prince led her to his Palace, and with great pomp and ceremony proclaimed her the new Ameera. Nonetheless, she continued to work on the coats for her brothers without once uttering a word.

And so, day followed day and everybody was happy; for everybody loved the new Ameera. All but the Vizier – a greedy grasping old man who secretly coveted the Prince's vast riches over which, in the absence of an heir, the Prince had graciously conceded him full authority.

But now that the Prince was married, thought the Vizier, and likely soon to have an heir, the situation was bound to change. And he, the now-all-important Vizier, would then have to step aside and relinquish all say and authority to the new young master.

The thought galled him. But was there no way out? Only one: the total elimination of the Ameera before she could give the Prince an heir.

On this murderous thought he spent nights and days, hatching plots and plans and how best to implement them. Meanwhile, he surreptitiously kept a close watch over the Ameera and all her movements, and he soon discovered that she was wont to steal quietly out of the Palace, late in the night, when the Prince and the Royal household had retired, and walk swiftly in the direction of the garden gates.

Cautiously he followed her. And though he made fully certain that she went no further than the precinct of the garden wall to pick a basketful of acacia leaves for the work on which she was continuously engaged, he cunningly started spreading the insidious rumour that the Ameera had a lover whom she secretly met late in the night by the Palace garden wall.

Before long, this rumour penetrated to the ears of the Prince (as the Vizier intended it to), and the Prince angrily demanded of him an explanation.

The Vizier put up a great show of indignation, and was abject in his apologies that the rumour should have reached the ears of the Prince. But, with a false pretence of loyalty to the Ameera, he declined to vouchsafe all further explanation.

This angered the Prince even more, and he threatened (as again the Vizier intended him to), that unless he was given a satisfactory explanation, he would have the Vizier beheaded for allowing such a rumour to spread.

So, in the face of such a grave threat to his life, what could the Vizier do but admit, with greatly feigned reluctance, that he himself had more than once seen the Ameera leave the Palace late in the night to keep her tryst by the garden wall?

To this grave accusation the Prince had not a word to say. He merely retired to his apartments, and that night – at the hour the Vizier had indicated, he stationed himself at one of the Palace windows from which, sure enough, he could clearly see the Ameera all veiled up steal softly out of the Palace and swiftly disappear in the wake of the garden wall.

Overwhelmed with grief and sorrow, yet unable to disregard this irrefutable proof of the Ameera's adultery, the Prince had no choice but to sentence her, like any other adulteress, to death by fire. And he authorized the Vizier to carry out the sentence.

The Vizier's jubilation was great. For that was precisely what he had schemed and plotted for.

Accordingly, early next morning, he had it publicly proclaimed that the Ameera was an adulteress, and that by order of the Prince she was to be thrown into a pit of fire at dusk that same day.

The Ameera heard the proclamation and longed to denounce the Vizier to the Prince, for she was fully aware of his evil machinations. But she knew that were she to utter a word, even though in defence of her honour and her life, she would jeopardize for ever the redemption of her brothers from the spell the step-mother had cast upon them.

She therefore allowed the Vizier's men to lead her out of the Palace into the market-place where she sat silently watching the preparations for her doom, and strove with redoubled efforts to complete before dusk the tenth coat on which she was already far advanced.

Meanwhile, the market-place was slowly filling up with people who came from far and near to watch the execution, and the Vizier's men assiduously occupied themselves in digging and preparing the pit of fire.

The late afternoon sun was now beginning to set, and the men applied the first match to the mound of kindling which was to set the piled up logs on fire. But no sooner did the kindling begin to catch and crackle, than ten white doves swooped down from the sky upon it, and with a fierce beat of their wings snuffed the fire out.

The Vizier's men shooed them off with great clamour and shouting, and tried again and again to start the fire going. But the doves gave them no chance, for every time the fire started to catch, they would swoop down upon it and snuff it out with the beat of their wings.

And so it went on, to the great delight of the crowd which filled the market-place, clapping and shouting and highly applauding the performance of the doves.

But the Vizier's men were frantic. The dusk of night was slowly falling, and not a log was yet afire. How would they explain to the Vizier – who would soon be coming to supervise the execution, their failure to carry out his orders?

Then, in the midst of all this commotion, the Ameera's father walked into the market-place. He had never ceased to harass the stepmother as to what had happened to his daughter. And when she finally informed him that the ugly girl he had chased out of his presence was none other than his daughter, he immediately set out to find her and take her back home.

Attracted, however, by the great commotion in the market-place, and little dreaming that the pit of fire which was then being prepared was intended for his daughter, he stood with the crowd curiously watching the fight between the Vizier's men and the ten white doves.

Finally, the Vizier's men succeeded in starting the fire, and this time the ten white doves did not attempt to snuff it out. Instead, they circled low above the Ameera, and she, having finally succeeded in completing her task, was able to fit each of them with a coat of acacia leaves as they lit one by one close to her, and they regained their human shape, this time never to lose it again.

Now the father who was not standing too far away, immediately recognized his ten lost sons and ran forward joyously to embrace them. He was then too close to the Ameera not to recognize in her his beautiful lost daughter too, for the spell the stepmother had cast upon her to make her look repulsive in her father's eyes, was but a temporary one and had soon worn off.

Meanwhile, with the doves out of the way, the pit of fire was now ablaze with flaming logs. So the Vizier's men approached the Ameera to tie her up and throw her into it. But the Ameera was now free to speak, and whilst her father and ten brothers stood firm guard around her, she demanded to see the Prince to whom she fully denounced the Vizier.

And the Prince who loved the Ameera dearly, needed no further proof of her probity. He was, moreover, so happy to hear her talk, that he invited her father and ten brothers to come and live with them permanently in the Palace, and gave orders for a second wedding to be held in great pomp and style to reinstate the Ameera as his lawful legal wife.

What of the Vizier? By order of the Prince he was bound hand and foot and thrown into the very pit of fire he had prepared for the Ameera.

Which brings to my mind a popular Sudanese saying:

> O you who dig the pit of evil,
> Widen its walls.
> You dig it for your innocent brother,
> Tomorrow into it you'll fall.

Hassan the physician

There was once a rich merchant, and he had three daughters whom he loved very dearly.

One day, before setting out on a long journey, he asked each of them what she would like him to bring her back from his travels.

The eldest said she would like a mirror which would show her the world; the second said she would like a pestle and mortar which could be heard clanging from East to West; but the third said she would like nothing other than her father's safe return.

The father however gruffly insisted that, like her sisters, his youngest daughter too should ask him for something. But hurt at the sharp manner in which her father spoke to her, the girl retired silently to her room and went to bed weeping.

Then she dreamed that an old woman came to her and said: 'Tomorrow morning, before your father sets off on his journey, he will again ask you what you would like him to bring you back from his travels. Tell him that you would like him to bring you back "him of the curly hair, from the land of happenings rare".'

So, next morning, when her father again posed to her

93

the question his youngest daughter told him precisely that. And the father, too preoccupied at the time to ponder this strange request, promised he would.

He then set off on his journey, travelled far and wide, and acquired a great variety of fine silks and rich brocades and rare spices. And when it was time for him to return home, he suddenly bethought himself of his youngest daughter's strange request. But search as he would, he could find no such person as 'him of the curly hair', or anyone who could indicate to him what or where was that 'land of happenings rare'.

So, having already acquired the mirror for his eldest daughter, and the pestle and mortar for his second daughter, he decided not to waste any more time on a futile search for his youngest daughter's strange request. Instead, to make up for any disappointment his failure to satisfy her wish might cause, he would let her have her pick of any of the many valuables he had acquired. And, with this thought in mind, he boarded a boat which was to take him home.

Shortly after the boat had set sail, however, a violent storm broke out. And the passengers, fearing a shipwreck, were soon asking one another who amongst them could have left a promise unfulfilled. The merchant had to admit it was he.

At that, they immediately forced him to land on an island they were by-passing, and as he sat distraught and dismayed by the waterfront, the islanders thronged around him and asked him what his trouble was.

He told them of his promise to his youngest daughter, and his inability to fulfil it. He then went on to deplore the unkind fate which had unleashed the storm, thus forcing him to land on that strange shore, far away from home.

But the islanders assured him that it was a kind fate which had unleashed the storm, thus forcing him to land on their island; for that was precisely the land of 'happenings rare' he was looking for. 'As to him of the curly hair, he is none other than our Prince, and he lives in that great Palace yonder,' they concluded, pointing to a beautiful white Palace which rose high on a hill in the middle of the island.

The merchant could hardly believe his good luck. He begged the islanders to take him to the Palace, and when he was ushered into the presence of the Prince, he laid out before him the choicest variety of his silks and spices. The Prince graciously accepted the gift, and asked the merchant what he would like in return.

The merchant then told him of his youngest daughter's wish, and earnestly begged the Prince to go and see her.

The Prince agreed to go. 'But I can only appear to her at fall of night, and through a fountain filled with orange-flower water,' he said to the merchant.

The merchant assured him that it would all be as he desired. And as soon as he was back home, he told his daughter of his encounter with the Prince, and bade her be ready to receive him at fall of night by a fountain filled with orange-flower water.

The girl was delighted. Joyfully she decked herself out in her gayest and prettiest, and anxious not to miss her Prince, sat by the water fountain long before fall of night. She sat and sat. . . .

Then, when the stars had one by one found their right place in the open heavens, a soft ripple broke the surface of the scented water, and the next moment the Prince emerged through – young, straight and handsome.

The girl hastened forward to meet him. And when he saw her he fell instantly in love with her, for she was as beautiful as the moon in its fourteenth night. They then lingered, hand in hand, happily together, and at break of dawn the Prince disappeared. But he came again the next night and every night thereafter.

Thus was the girl in the seventh heaven of happiness.

eric fraser

But her happiness aroused the bitter envy of her two elder sisters, and between them they connived to wreck it.

So, secretly one night, just before their younger sister came to sit by the fountain, they threw several handfuls of finely crushed glass into it. And when the Prince came to emerge through, the glass cut him cruelly all over. He then immediately disappeared.

The girl waited for him all that night, and all the nights that followed. But he never came. Sad and forlorn she went about the house deploring the loss of her Prince, and wondering what could have happened to him.

Her father did his best to comfort her. But her sisters brutally told her that it was obvious the Prince had tired of her, and that therefore she should learn to forget him.

Deep down within her, however, the girl was convinced that nothing short of a serious impediment could have prevented the Prince from coming to see her. And, one day, when she felt she could wait no longer, she decided to go and look for him. So, she filled her purse with money, and her food bag with provisions, and set forth in quest of her lover.

Day after day she walked, making enquiries here, there, and everywhere. But all to no avail. Then, one evening, as she sat resting under the spreading branches of a fig-tree, two doves came to perch upon it. And, with a soft flutter of wings, one said to the other:

'What's the latest down your way, sister?'

'Haven't you heard?' said the other. 'Him of the curly hair hasn't much longer to live.'

'And great is the pity,' said the first, 'so young, so handsome. . . . Is there no cure for him?'

'Softly, softly,' cautioned the second. 'His cure lies in our death. . . .'

'How so?' came the fearful query.

'I tell you . . . nothing but our two hearts and two

livers plucked live out of us, then roasted and pounded into a smooth mixture for smearing all over his body, would restore him to life.'

'Coo-oo!' softly breathed the first dove, and with a thankful flutter of wings for the safe security of their perch, both doves then settled down to sleep.

The girl who heard every word of this dialogue, waited until the night was at its darkest. Then she crept quietly up the tree and caught the two doves. Deftly she plucked out their hearts and livers, and when she had roasted these over a hastily assembled twig fire, she pounded them into a smooth paste which she then packed between two large fig leaves.

Early next morning she disguised herself as a man, and hastened to the waterfront where she boarded a boat which took her to the Prince's island.

The islanders hardly noticed her; for they were silently mourning the grave illness of their Prince. But to attract attention, the girl walked through the streets loudly proclaiming that she was: 'Hassan, a physician of skills who is able to cure all ills.'

The islanders heard her and suddenly came to life. Then, without so much as by your leave, they rushed her off to the Palace where all the physicians and magicians who had desperately tried, but sadly failed, to cure the Prince, sat together, resignedly waiting for the end.

With one accord, and without any loss of time, they ushered the disguised girl into the Prince's bedroom, and she immediately set to work smearing her precious ointment on his festering sores and wounds. After that she sat patiently by his bedside the rest of that day and all through the night.

Next morning, to her great secret joy, and the people's candid astonishment at such a miraculous change, the sores had considerably healed, and at eventide after yet another application of the precious ointment, the flesh began to knit healthily together.

On the third day the Prince was well enough to get out of bed and ask for food and drink. The people's joy was great. And the Prince was so grateful to Hassan the Physician for having restored him to life, that he offered to pay him any fee he named. But Hassan would not accept any fee.

'All I would like,' he said to the Prince, 'is for us both to share together a dish of *asseda bi-asal* (some sort of porridge with honey), and for you to tell me how you came by those sores and wounds.'

The Prince ordered a large dish of *asseda bi-asal*, and as he and his Physician sat face to face eating it together, he told his story.

'What I cannot understand,' he finally concluded, 'is why she should have done this to me. I loved her, and had every intention of marrying her. . . .'

'And now?' interposed Hassan eagerly.

'Now, I am going to seek her out – possibly this very night, and take my revenge for the cruel way in which she has treated me.'

With that, the two parted.

The girl was now in no doubt that it was her two sisters who had thrown the crushed glass into the fountain, and when she returned home, she bitterly accused them of conniving to wreck her happiness. Shamefacedly, they admitted their guilt. She then thoroughly cleaned out the water fountain, and filled it afresh with sparkling orange-flower water in readiness for the Prince.

Sure enough, soon after the fall of night, he emerged through, straight and handsome as ever before. Then, without giving him time to utter a word, the girl went up to him and said:

'I conjure you by the Physician Hassan, with whom you have eaten *asseda bi-asal*, listen to me and I will tell you what has happened.'

The Prince thus knew that it was she who had saved his life, and that she had never, at any time, meant to harm him. So he carried her off to the 'land of happenings rare, where they had sons and daughters fair, and lived happily together for ever after.'

Hassan the brave

There was once a woman and she had a son who was the apple of her eye. His name was Hassan. And he was so strong and fearless, that all those who knew him nicknamed him Hassan the Brave.

Hassan was very proud of his nickname. And every morning when he awoke, he would flex his muscles and expand his chest, then turn to his mother and say: 'Am I not the bravest of the brave, mother?' And the mother would proudly reply: 'Indeed you are, my son.'

One day, a neighbour who had no children and was very envious of Hassan's mother, said to her: 'Next time your son asks you if he is the bravest of the brave, to save him having a swollen head, tell him: "Eve's progeny is numerous, and the world is prosperous, my son".'

The woman did as her neighbour advised, and the next morning when Hassan put to her his customary question, she said to him: 'Eve's progeny is numerous, and the world is prosperous, my son.'

'In other words, you no more think I am the bravest of the brave, mother,' Hassan said to her. 'Very well then. I shall go out into the world, and if I find anyone braver than I am, I shall not return.'

In vain did the mother try to dissuade him from so doing; Hassan would not be deflected from his purpose. He strapped on his sword and filled his saddlebags with provisions, and after saying good-bye to his mother, he set out on his horse to find out if there was anyone stronger or braver than he.

On he rode and on. And by early afternoon he came to a small clearing in the middle of the desert where he saw from a discreet distance two men: one was riding a lion, and the other was riding a tiger.

'Aha!' thought Hassan, reining in his horse. 'Those two are assuredly braver than I am, for one is riding a lion, and the other is riding a tiger; whilst I am merely riding a horse.'

After pondering this for a while, he decided to find out more about the two men from a closer range. So he dismounted, and leading his horse behind him, he approached them on foot with the customary greetings: 'As-salamu aleikum!'

'Aleikum as-salam!' the men replied, dismounting in turn, and stepping forward to meet him. They then invited him to rest himself and his mount until the heat of the day was over. Hassan accepted their invitation, and the three of them sat and chatted pleasantly together in the cool shade of a cluster of date-palms.

Then, when the late afternoon sun began to slant behind a sand dune, Hassan, not wishing to be caught in an awkward place by the fall of night, considered it was time to move on.

He asked his companions if they intended riding on any further that day, but they told him that they intended to remain in the clearing for a few more days, and take it in turn to hunt for food and bake their bread. Wouldn't Hassan like to join them? And Hassan who could have wished for no better opportunity to test his strength and bravery against theirs, gladly accepted.

Accordingly, next day he was detailed to go hunting for food, whilst the tiger-rider went in search of firewood, and the lion-rider stayed behind to bake the bread.

In the evening, however, when Hassan returned from his hunting, shortly followed by the tiger-rider, there was no bread awaiting them.

'How come there is no bread?' Hassan asked the lion-rider.

'Oh,' replied the lion-rider, 'I had it all hot and ready for our meal, when a hungry old man came by and begged me to give it to him.'

'A very commendable act of charity,' said Hassan cheerfully. But the tiger-rider made no comment.

On the second day Hassan was again detailed to go hunting for food, whilst this time the lion-rider went in search of firewood, and the tiger-rider stayed behind to bake the bread.

But once again when the two men returned in the evening, there was no bread awaiting them.

'What happened to the bread this time?' queried Hassan.

'Oh,' replied the tiger-rider, 'I had it all hot and ready to serve, when the same hungry old man came by and begged me to give it to him.'

'A very commendable act of charity,' said Hassan again. But the lion-rider made no comment.

On the third day it was Hassan's turn to stay behind and bake the bread, whilst the other two went off, one to hunt for food, the other to search for firewood.

So, Hassan set to in good time to bake the bread. Carefully he measured out the flour, and when he had worked a dough to the right consistency, he patted a loaf into shape and popped it to bake on a crackling woodfire.

Soon the desert air was filled with the appetising aroma of baking bread, and Hassan sniffed it hungrily. 'It smells good and should taste good,' he thought, as he drew the loaf out of the fire. 'But this time,' he firmly vowed to himself, 'that hungry old man will not have a crumb of it!'

But it wasn't a hungry old man who came begging for the bread. It was a great big black giant who emerged through a great big black hole in the ground and demanded of Hassan the whole loaf.

Hassan looked at the giant in mild surprise. 'So *you* are the hungry old man that comes to appropriate the bread every evening, are you?'

'That is correct,' affirmed the giant. 'And if you are wise, you will hand over that loaf as readily as your two companions have done; otherwise, you are in trouble.'

'But I welcome trouble,' was Hassan's cheerful retort. 'Therefore I refuse to hand over the loaf.'

'Then I will just have to kill you,' said the giant taking a threatening lunge forward.

But Hassan was quick with his sword. And before the giant could lay hands on him, he cut off his head.

'Ha-ha!' mocked the giant, as a second head instantly sprang on his shoulders. 'You didn't know I have more than one head, did you?'

'And you didn't know I have more than one sword,' riposted Hassan, wielding a second sword and cutting off the giant's second head.

'Ha-ha!' again mocked the giant, as a third head instantly appeared on his shoulders. 'As you see, I have more than two heads.'

'And as you see, I have more than two swords,' retorted Hassan, as he swung a third sword and cut off the giant's third head.

And so the duel continued, until Hassan had cut off six of the giant's heads. When he had cut off the seventh, the giant lunged forward and fell heavily on the ground – stone dead.

Cautiously Hassan approached the headless body, and as he turned it over, he noticed a prominent swelling in the dead giant's left calf. He slit it open, and therein found a small glass case with seven live green birds in it. He had just time to slip the case in his pocket, when his

eric fraser

two companions returned from their day's hunt, and promptly asked for bread.

Hassan offered it to them. And as they sat, silent and shamefaced, eating it, he pointed to the headless body of the giant and said with cold disdain: 'There lies the hungry old man who came begging you for bread every evening.'

The men hung their heads low and made no comment. 'And now that we have got rid of him,' proceeded Hassan, 'let us investigate the world from which he came. I will go first, in case of any likely danger. . . .'

But here to cover up for their cowardice in failing to face up to the giant and kill him, both men cried out simultaneously: 'No, no! We will go first and face up to any likely danger.'

'Each one in turn then,' said Hassan, as he slipped a rope round the lion-rider and lowered him down the hole. Half-way through, however, he began to shout: 'Fire! Fire! Pull me up, quick!'

Hassan pulled him up. He then tied the tiger-rider to the rope, and lowered him down the hole. But half-way through, he too began to shout: 'Fire! Fire! Pull me up, quick!'

Hassan pulled him up too. It was now his turn to go down the hole. So his two companions tied him to the rope and lowered him down. Half-way through he felt the fire, but he shouted: 'Keep lowering me down, faster, faster. . . .' And when he finally reached the bottom, he found himself in the courtyard of a palatial mansion where the water fountains were in full play, and the air was cool and soft.

Hassan freed himself from the rope and walked through the rooms of the mansion, lost in admiration of their richness, and wondering what king or genie of the lower world dwelt in them.

Presently the sound of faint moaning fell on his ears,

and guided by it, he came to a small chamber in which a beautiful young girl lay bound and strapped to her bed.

Cautiously Hassan approached the bed and asked: 'Are you an *ins,* or a *gins*?' (a human being or a genie?)

'I am very much an *ins*,' said the girl. 'And it was a cruel black giant who snatched me from my father's home in the world above, and brought me down here to force me to marry him. But I refuse to surrender to his wishes. That is why he beats me every night, and then straps me to the bed the next day to make sure I do not escape.'

Hassan freed the girl and assured her that the cruel black giant would trouble her no more, for he had just killed him in the world above, to which he would now take her back.

The girl was so grateful to Hassan that she showed him the secret cache where the giant kept all his riches, and helped him fill as many sacks as he could carry with nuggets of pure gold and precious stones.

When the sacks were ready, Hassan tied them one by one to his end of the rope, and signalled to the men above to haul them up. He then tied the girl, and when she too was safely hauled up, it was his turn to follow. But his erstwhile companions, now finding themselves in possession of such fabulous riches, and a beautiful girl to boot, cut the rope half-way up, and sent him careering back to the lower world.

The impact of his fall was so great, that he sank deeper into yet a lower world where all the people sat weeping and mourning. Hassan wanted to know the reason why. And he was told that the Jinn of the Sea, who was in the habit of claiming every year a beautiful young maiden for a bride, was coming that day to claim the King's daughter, for it was her turn to be sacrificed.

Hassan then asked to be led to the King's daughter, and he found her sitting alone, disconsolate and weeping, by the water's edge, waiting for the Jinn of the Sea to come and claim her.

He sat next to her and tried to comfort her. The girl thanked him and begged him to go away or the Jinn would kill him. But Hassan merely laughed. Then he pillowed his head on her lap and asked her to wake him up as soon as she saw the Jinn appear. After that, he fell into a snooze.

The girl stroked his hair and caressed his face, for he was young and handsome and very desirable. Presently she caught sight of the Jinn who was rapidly approaching, and she began to cry. Her tears rolled down her cheeks and dropped on Hassan's face, thus waking him up. 'Run for your life,' she begged, 'else he'll kill you.' But Hassan drew his sword and stood his ground.

'Leave my bride alone, Hassan,' menaced the Jinn as he splashed out of the sea.

For an answer Hassan swung his sword and struck at the Jinn's head. It remained unscathed. Again he swung his sword and struck. But again he failed to remove the Jinn's head.

'You are wasting your time, Hassan,' derided the Jinn, 'for I cannot die like other mortals. My life is not in my body.'

'In that case I am a dead man,' conceded Hassan, 'for I am entirely at your mercy. But since I am going to die and will not have a chance to divulge your secret, won't you tell me where your life lies?'

'It lies in seven little green live birds encased in the calf of a big black giant who lives in a world above this one,' said the Jinn boastfully.

At that Hassan suddenly recalled the little glass case with the seven green live birds he had extricated from the calf of the black giant he had killed, and begging the Jinn for a few moments respite to commend his soul to his Maker, he half turned his back, and drawing the glass case out of his pocket, surreptitiously throttled the seven little green birds.

No sooner had he done that, than with a fearful splash the Jinn fell back lifeless into the sea. And the people who were watching it all from a safe distance, now rushed forward to Hassan, shouting, cheering, and praising him for his great courage and bravery. They then carried him shoulder high to the King who was so grateful to him for saving his daughter's life, that he offered her to him as a bride, together with half his kingdom. But Hassan declined both offers.

'All I would ask of you,' he said to the King, 'is to use your power and influence to take me back to the world above. That is where I belong.'

'I will do that,' said the King. And, summoning forthwith his most able sorcerers and magicians, he ordered them to devise ways and means to carry out Hassan's wish.

The sorcerers and magicians sat up all night, burning incense and reciting prayers and incantations, and at dawn they bound Hassan's eyes and sat him on the wings of an enchanted eagle which carried him through seven lower worlds up to the world above.

There he found the lion-rider and the tiger-rider in hot dispute as to who should have the girl and the bigger share of the riches. He killed them both. Then he took the girl and the riches and went back to his mother who was praying day and night for her son's safe return.

Next morning when he awoke, he flexed his muscles and expanded his chest, and said to his mother: 'Am I not the bravest of the brave, mother?'

And this time the mother had no hesitation in saying: 'Indeed you are, my son.'

And so, tended, bended, the tale is ended.

Karakosh and Goha

Having now come to the end of my narrative, I feel that this collection of folk-tales would not be complete without the addition of a couple of anecdotes on two popular characters in the folklore of the Sudan and Egypt.

One is Karakosh, that much-dreaded Supreme Judge whose biased judgement and crooked sense of fair justice is a parable.

The other, is Goha, that much-quoted clown and jester whose sharp wit and quick repartee are proverbial.

Of Karakosh, the story goes that one day as he was walking incognito through the streets of the city, he saw a man carrying an oven-ready turkey in a tray, and followed him to a bakery.

He then heard the man instruct the baker to roast the turkey and have it ready for him by a certain hour when he would return to collect it.

The baker promised to do so. But no sooner did the man leave the bakery, than Karakosh went up to the baker and said to him:

'I am Karakosh. And I fancy this turkey for my dinner. So, when it is ready, be sure to have it sent to the Palace for me.'

'Very well, my Lord,' said the baker. 'But what am I to tell the rightful owner of the turkey when he returns to claim it?'

'Tell him,' said Karakosh, 'that you were on the point of popping the turkey into the oven, when it suddenly sprouted wings and flew out of the bakery.'

'I hear and obey, my Lord,' said the baker, 'but such talk would still not exonerate me from punishment.'

'Have no fear,' said Karakosh. 'I am the Supreme

Judge, and when your case comes before me, I shall clear you of all charges.'

Having thus had Karakosh's assurance that he would suffer no punishment, the baker proceeded to roast the turkey, and when it was ready he had it sent to the Judge's Palace.

In due course, the owner of the turkey returned to collect it. And the baker said to him:

'I regret to tell you, mate, that I was on the point of popping your turkey into the oven, when it suddenly sprouted wings and flew out of the bakery.'

'Sprouted wings and flew out of the bakery! A dead turkey! What kind of talk is this? You take me for a fool? You thief! You swindler!' shouted the man angrily, and he punched and kicked the baker all over.

The baker defended himself as best he could. Then he picked up a stone and aimed it at the man. But the man dodged, and the stone went whizzing past him to land with a hard thud on the ear of a fellow who was sleeping peacefully on the ground opposite the bakery, and killed him.

Immediately, the dead fellow's brother sprang upon the baker raining more kicks and punches upon him, and again the baker put up a valiant fight in self-defence. Then, thinking he had caught his assailant with all defences down, he drew back his arm and swung it out in what he intended to be a crippling punch on the jaw. But he missed his aim and the punch landed fair and square on the belly of a pregnant woman, who was standing watching the fight, causing her to miscarry on the spot.

Thereat, the woman's husband leaped upon the baker clawing, punching and kicking him, and the baker who now felt he could take no more corporal punishment, decided to end his life.

So, he made a desperate dash for the nearest mosque,

and threw himself from the top of the minaret. But instead of falling on the ground, he fell on a man who was walking peacefully along the street, and instantly killed him.

In a trice, the crowd who had witnessed the accident, closed in on the baker, and the dead man's brother fell upon him, waving his arms aloft, and shouting high for vengeance.

The baker saw he was now trapped. And his one thought was to flee. But where to flee. . . ? And how to flee. . . ? Wildly his eyes raked the crowd for the smallest possible outlet, and then hovered for a fleeting second on the hindparts of a donkey. Allah! Thou art indeed Great. . . !

With a prodigious lunge forward, the baker reached the donkey and then grabbed its tail with both hands. And the donkey, thus rudely jolted out of its asinine wits, bolted off with him in a loud bray of protest, scattering the crowd right and left in its headlong flight.

'Allah! Thou art indeed Great!' again breathed the baker, as he hung grimly on to the donkey's tail and watched with great relief the distance between him and his pursuers grow wider and wider.

Suddenly the tail came clean off in his hands, and whilst the donkey now all at once rid of the drag on his hindparts, halted abruptly in its tracks to work this phenomenon out, the crowd which was hot in pursuit behind, caught up with the baker and again fell mercilessly upon him, pounding, punching and kicking on all sides.

Finally, assailants and assaulted found their way to the Court of Law, and stood before Judge Karakosh who opened the session by cross-examining the owner of the turkey: 'And why did you assault the baker, my man?'

'Because, my Lord, I gave him a turkey to roast for me, and when I went to claim it, he had the nerve to tell me that the turkey had suddenly sprouted wings and flown out of the bakery.'

'And is it not in the power of Almighty Allah to return a dead turkey to life?' challenged Karakosh.

The owner of the turkey looked at him tongue-tied. 'But you seem to be in doubt as to the power of Almighty Allah to revive the dead,' proceeded Karakosh coolly; 'for that, I sentence you to sixty strokes of the birch and a sixty-dinar fine.'

Next came the brother of the man who was killed by a stone. 'And you,' said Karakosh to him, 'why did you assault the baker?'

'Because, my Lord, he killed my brother who was sleeping peacefully on the ground opposite the bakery, by aiming at him a large stone which landed on his ear.'

'Did your brother bleed?' queried Karakosh.

'No, my Lord.'

'Did you feel his pulse?'

'No, my Lord.'

'Then how can you prove that it was the baker who killed him, since he neither bled, nor did you feel his pulse? He may well have been dead long before the stone hit him. I therefore find you guilty of assault and sentence you to sixty strokes of the birch, and a sixty-dinar fine.'

It was now the turn of the man whose wife had miscarried, and Karakosh said to him: 'And why did you assault the baker, my man?'

'Because, my Lord, he punched my pregnant wife on the belly, causing her to miscarry on the spot.'

'In that case,' said Karakosh, 'I rule that the baker take your wife now, and return her to you pregnant as she was before he caused her to miscarry.'

'Never!' shouted the man outraged. 'Absolutely never, my Lord! Such a condition is utterly unacceptable!'

'In that case,' said Karakosh, 'since you will not accept this equitable reparation, 'I find you guilty of assault, and sentence you to sixty strokes of the birch, and a sixty-dinar fine.'

Finally, he turned to the brother of the second man who was killed and said to him: 'And why did you assault the baker, my man?'

'Because, my Lord, he threw himself from the top of the minaret, and fell like a thunderbolt on my brother who was walking peacefully along the street, and killed him.'

'In that case,' said Karakosh, 'I rule that the baker be made to walk along the street, and that you go up the minaret and throw yourself down upon him, and so kill him as he has killed your brother.'

'But, my Lord,' protested the baker, 'what guarantee have I that instead of falling on the baker, I do not fall on the ground and so kill myself in my attempt to kill him?'

'That is a chance you have to take,' said Karakosh. 'But since you do not seem to be willing to take it, I find you guilty of assault, and sentence you to sixty strokes of the birch, and a sixty-dinar fine.'

There now remained the owner of the donkey who had led his mount to Court in the hope that Judge Karakosh would uphold his claim for compensation to the loss of its tail. But having heard the judgement passed on his predecessors, his hopes were now dashed, and he was hurriedly sneaking out of Court when Karakosh caught sight of him and called out peremptorily: 'You there! Come back here. Why did you assault the baker?'

'I haven't assaulted the baker in any way, my Lord,' said the man, meekly retracing his steps.

'Then why are you here? And' (as his eye fell on the animal's shorn behind) 'what happened to your donkey's tail?'

'Nothing . . . nothing at all, my Lord. This donkey never had a tail . . . it was born tail-less.'

Of Goha, we are told that he once had a neighbour who was anxious to go off on a short vacation. But he had twenty geese and no one to look after them for him during his absence. So he thought of going over to Goha and asking him if he would be so kind as to look after the geese for him during his absence.

'Willingly,' said Goha, 'but it would help if you could bring the geese over to my own backyard where I can feed and water them without having to go across to yours.'

'With pleasure,' said the neighbour, and early next morning he drove his flock of geese into Goha's backyard. 'Here we are, Goha, twenty geese in all,' he said, and off he went.

When he returned, he went over to Goha to claim his twenty geese. To his consternation, however, Goha returned to him nineteen geese only.

'But Goha,' protested the neighbour, 'I am one goose short. I left you twenty geese; these are only nineteen.'

'My friend,' said Goha complacently, 'I have never been able to work out figures. All I know is that you drove a flock of geese into my backyard one morning, and asked me to look after them for you. I did so. Here they are now, all yours for the taking.'

In vain did the neighbour protest and argue that he was still one goose short. Goha could just not see it. Finally, the neighbour took himself and his geese to Court, and registered a complaint against Goha with the Cadi.

The Cadi summoned Goha to Court and asked him why he had witheld one goose from the twenty his neighbour had confided to his care.

'Your Worship,' said Goha, 'I have never been able to understand figures. All I know is that my neighbour here drove a flock of geese into my backyard one morning, and asked me to look after them for him during his absence on a vacation. I did so. Now he claims he is one goose short. I just don't understand how he has come to this conclusion.'

The Cadi, a benign old man, felt for Goha, and tried to help him out of his mathematical difficulty. So he called for twenty soldiers, and when they stood lined up along the wall of the Courtroom, he turned to Goha, and said:

'Now Goha, I will show you how your neighbour came to the conclusion that he is one goose short. We have here as many soldiers as the number of geese your neighbour claims to have left with you. Do you follow?'

'I do, Your Worship,' said Goha.

'Now,' pursued the Cadi. 'If we have as many soldiers as we have geese, it stands to reason that there should be one goose for each soldier. Correct?'

'Correct, Your Worship.'

The Cadi then ordered each soldier to pick up a goose from the number which was let loose before them. Nineteen soldiers each picked up a goose, but the twentieth remained empty-handed.

'You see, Goha,' said the Cadi turning to him hopefully, 'each of these soldiers picked up a goose, but there is one who remained empty-handed. Can you tell me why?'

'Because,' was the prompt retort, 'begging Your Worship's pardon, the man is a dunce. The geese were all there before him, why didn't he pick up one?'